Fast Jack Rose

Ghost Gatherer

Raymond H. Stem II

PublishAmerica
Baltimore

ISBN: 978-1-4489-4250-3
PUBLISHED BY PUBLISHAMERICA, LLLP
www.publishamerica.com
Baltimore

Printed in the United States of America

Part I
The Overture

Chapter One

The story of a remarkable life began in 1854, when a penniless twelve year old Irish immigrant named Robert John "Jack" Rose landed in the New World. His parents, Sean and Molly begged a position for him as an apprentice deckhand in return for his passage on a sailing ship bound for America just weeks before they were to die from starvation. They were just two more tear drops in the ocean of grief caused when God visited upon the Irish the twin plagues of the potato famine and the English. The crops that didn't die in the field were taken back to Britain by callous English landlords leaving the Irish to eat grass or nothing at all.

Being a good Irish Catholic, the first thing he did was to find a church and give thanks for a safe arrival as he had promised his mother he would do. He also gave thanks for his life's blessings, although anyone else would have been hard pressed to discern any. For an Irish Catholic in the 1850's, merely waking up in the morning was often the sum total of that day's blessings. Centuries earlier, that hated English bastard Oliver Cromwell, decreed that being Irish was an abomination and being Catholic compounded the crime. It would seem that God was a Cromwell partisan.

Because of his willingness to do just about any job regardless of wretchedness, the ship's captain offered him fulltime employment. He didn't have the strength of an adult man, but he had more eagerness and available sweat than any three seamen. He respectfully declined the offer stating he felt a better future could be secured on shore.

That future began poorly after he landed in New Orleans and learned burying Yellow Fever victims was the only job allowed a brand new American, late of Ireland. The place was awash in slaves, but they were far too valuable to be risked on such a plague. Everyone knew that was why God had created the Irish in the first place.

For a boy born and raised in the damp chill of Ireland, the heat and humidity of south Louisiana was oppressively overpowering even for one as young and vigorous as Jack. After a few days, he threw down his shovel and walked off. He kept walking until he reached Texas. He had heard tales from the men on the docks of the prosperity to be found in cattle towns and the nearby ranches. It was said that one could even make as much as thirty dollars and found per month. He didn't know for sure, but he doubted his father had never earned such a sum for any entire year of his life.

After nearly eight weeks of walking, living hand-to-mouth by doing whatever odd jobs he could find, he caught on with one of the smaller spreads near Rock Wall. Billy O'Brian, the owner was impressed at the effort he had given just the get there. He was a redheaded son of Eire himself and said Jackie looked like he may be a long-lost relative so he could hardly do otherwise. His wife, Sinead agreed and offered to educate "this lovely lad from Cork." Her bona fides being a successful matriculation from the convent school in Galway before immigration.

He worked hard and learned well and after a few years he had become a decent cowhand and what passed for a fairly educated young man of the times. Thanks to the O'Brian's old world accents, there was no chance possible of him ever losing his Irish brogue. However the lessons he absorbed most eagerly were supplied by Theo Johns, a former gunfighter and sometime lawman from Fort Worth. Johns taught him to shoot well but the two most important lessons he imparted were being accurate was far more crucial than just being fast. He drilled into Jack's head that if he couldn't hit a man, it didn't matter how quick he was, he was going to be one who was dead. The second was a man must be resolute of purpose and fully committed in order to stare down and shoot someone about to kill him. Standing in front of one who has lethal intentions, a man must have supreme confidence in his own ability to thwart those intentions. A dead man has no further intentions.

He worked diligently and became most proficient. He worked even harder until his speed matched his skill level. He was on the way to becoming as able as Johns himself. He was becoming more than a mere facsimile of the man he idolized; he was becoming something of an attraction in his own right. The ranch hands enjoyed the competition between the two men and would wager on who was the fastest and most accurate. Eventually Johns conceded that Jack was discernibly the better of the two. One afternoon after losing one of their contests, Johns smiled and said, "Red, you remind me of me at your age, except I was taller!" Both men laughed and bathed before heading to town to drink up Jack's winnings.

That fateful night while together in a saloon, he displayed his most valuable attribute—he had the nerve of Nero! A drunken drifter recognized Johns as the man who had killed his brother. He pulled his gun and then shouted for Johns to turn and face him. He fired as Johns looked up, killing him instantly. The drifter still had his pistol aimed in Jack's direction when he pulled his own gun and shot him in the heart. His reputation was born at that instant. He had drawn and killed a man who had a pistol already pointed at him. As the night's drinking continued, witnesses swore that Jack had drawn, fired and holstered his gun before the dead man hit the floor. One drunk expanded the story when he claimed that actually Jack drew, fired and holstered his gun before the bullet even hit its target!

But he didn't hear any of the silly comments because he was taking the terrible news back to the ranch. He was distraught as he told the boss and the other hands what had happened. He kept

RAYMOND H. STEM II

blaming himself for not being more alert to the movements of a hate-filled angry man. Several of the hands kept telling him that he was not experienced enough to have even known what to have looked for. The boss added that since he was in the very first real gunfight he had ever seen, there was nothing he could have done differently.

But he vowed that things would indeed be forever different. Theo Johns had taught him to draw and to shoot, but the death of Theo Johns taught him the greatest lesson of all—to always survey the mood and movements of armed men. If a man looks dangerous, he probably is but if a man looks nervous, there must be a reason. A dangerous man reacts to threats he sees in front of him, while a terrified man reacts to threats he sees in his head. Of the two, the latter is by far the more frighteningly lethal because a scared man will do anything to protect himself including shooting another in the back.

The story of his extraordinary feat quickly made the rounds. His boss paid him off and advised him, for his own benefit to leave the area before every gun-hand around could show up to challenge themselves by pitting their skills against his in man's deadliest competition. Billy and Sinead were heartbroken to lose someone who had been a son to them, but they would rather see him go and possibly survive than stay and possibly not. They could never have endured witnessing the latter. He had gathered his first ghost and reluctantly said his goodbyes to the only family he had had in many years, or would have for many more and rode away into the rest of his life.

Chapter Two

After the War Between the States, thousands of emotionally broken men searched for their lost humanity. Many hundred of these men, mainly those who had worn the Grey and no longer had a home to return to, simply lost interest in being human. They traded on the only skill an army hones in men—the skill to kill other men. These men soon found the gangs of still wanted deserters, bounty hunters, Mexican bandits and homegrown gunfighters to unite into the Devil's own idea of evilness.

It was these evil men that Judge Bob Shafer of El Paso feared would soon make his town unlivable if not handled decisively. He needed a force feared by these men to stop the easy flow back and forth from havens across the border. He decided that what he needed was someone with the ability to convince these men that they were safer in Mexico. He sent for the one man who met these requirements perfectly.

While he waited, the judge looked out of his second floor window of the federal courthouse at the bustling street below. It hadn't rained in a week and the mud streets had started to dry, solidifying the ruts into hardened grooves that captured the wheels of wagons and buggies forcing the vehicles into inescapable tracks akin to that of the railroads. He smiled as he watched wagon after wagon travel a few yards then jerk sideways as they found the trenches before continuing onward.

A group of a dozen men rode slowly into view, stopped, dismounted, and entered the saloon directly across the street. As each approached the swinging doors of the establishment, they slowed and looked both ways up and down the boardwalks. The last man even turned completely around and entered backwards. The judge muttered aloud to himself, "What are you looking for boy? What 'cha got on your mind that you're so scared shitless something may be following you? You ain't got mischief on your mind, now do ya?"

As he watched the nervous men, his court clerk knocked and entered the office and informed him that the man he had summoned was in the outer office waiting. His last thought as he watched the man enter the establishment was, "It's good you're wary you sons-of-bitches because what you're scared of is here now."

By 1871, the twenty-nine year old "Fast Jack" Rose had become the most feared pistol-fighter on the border. He had gathered the ghost's of fifteen men when the judge decided to use him before there came a time he was forced to hang him. To the judge, Jack was the special man with singular skills for which he sought as the bulwark against any of these dangerous men thinking of visiting their mischief upon his town.

Jack sat in the judge's outer office trying to decide why the man had sent for him. He hadn't been arrested, merely summoned. He hadn't been charged with anything lately that he knew of. In the eyes of the law, he had never started any of his fights since he was always exonerated at trial when witnesses, terrified at retribution if he were set free, testified the other man always tried to draw first, which for the most part was usually true. He never purposely intimidated a witness, but his reputation did. Most of these did not know that he would never harm an innocent bystander because he was not that kind of man. He was scary as hell, but upright.

As he sat stumped, the judge stood at the door and motioned him inside the inner office and indicated for him to sit.

"Jack...I may call you Jack?" the judge asked.

He grinned widely and said, "Sir, you're the man with the power to be hangin' me at your leisure, so how much of an objection could I possibly be makin'?"

Continuing, the judge said, "As you know, it can be dangerous around here and the level of violent gunplay is on the rise. West Texas is a good place with good people, and these good people deserve to be safe from these lawless bastards who get drunk and shoot up the place when the mood hits them just right! The local sheriff and deputies are becoming overwhelmed by the number of murdering scum, especially from across the border. So what we need around here is a new way of doing things. What we need around here is someone that scares the be-Jesus out of these lawless bastards. What we need around here is you Jack. So what do you say my boy? Do you want to be on this side of the law for a change? Do you want to be working for me, or keep worrying about me?"

He sat quiet for a moment trying to get a grasp on what he had just heard, "Judge, I ain't real sure what you just said. Are you askin' me to go up against these bastards as a lawman?"

"Precisely! Well of a sort anyway. Basically, I want you to be a one-man border guard, kind of like a badass gate keeper, keeping the riffraff in Mexico and out of the great state of By God Texas! Here at the border between El Paso and Juarez there's agencies on both sides doing their best to handle things, but there's hundreds of miles of unguarded border where sinister sons-of-bitches can wade across unnoticed and wreak havoc. It's these characters that interest me the most, if you follow. The army can't do it for two reasons; first they patrol in great wads of blue and their dust can be seen for miles so the bad sorts merely hide until they pass, and second, they couldn't find shit in an outhouse anyway! This new Yankee army just ain't all that sharp as far as I can tell. So what do you say? I ain't got all day, there's folks wanting to get hung this morning."

"Let's see if I got this right. You want me to be a deputy whose job is to kill murdering scum tryin' to cross the border? Damn, judge is that legal?"

The judge starting to rile, "Damned right, it's legal if I say it's legal, and I say it's legal! I don't mean just go around shooting folks willy-nilly; only those you know for a fact deserve it. Of course you could always warn them first for the proprieties," he winked, "it's up to you, but I wouldn't give these pigs much notice other than the sound of a gunshot if it was me. So what's it to be?"

In keeping with his impulsive personality, he said, "I wouldn't think of goin' against a judge's order, so I guess I'm your man," he said. Like most events in his life, he had made a snap decision. He was philosophically adverse to reasoned introspection. He almost never put much more thought than this behind his actions because he felt life should be no more complicated than the search for a good steak or a bad woman.

"Good! Stand up and raise your right hand, 'Do you Jack Rose solemnly swear to uphold the laws of The United States of America by killin' them that need killin' so help you God?'"

"Yes sir!"

"Say 'I do' damn it!"

"I do…damn it!" he grinned.

The judge pulled a badge from his drawer and tossed it to Jack and told him to wear it where it would be seen, then he added, "I ain't got the funds to guard and feed many prisoners so don't arrest none, unless of course, they have a large bounty on their head. Ah hell, not even then! Just tie their bodies across their horse and I'll handle it from here."

The judge went to the corner of the room and retrieved the rifle leaning there and said, "This is the latest Sharps .52 caliber rifle and the only tool you'll get from me. It was left by a fella who came down from Colorado. Had to hang him, too bad really, good boy, kinda liked him. Couldn't let it go to rust, so here. It can blow the head off a Billy Goat at eight hundred yards and here's a box of cartridges to get you started. When you use these up, you buy the next. God's speed and by the way, that badge will tell everybody I made you a deputy, but don't tell nobody what I said about how you should do your job. Understand?" The judge didn't want the public to know of his part in this nefarious plan since it was questionably legal and unquestionably unethical. He just hoped that it would be effective. It was, for all practical purposes, a "shoot on sight" license to kill. The only thing separating Jack and the men he sought was the badge. The judge mused, "Now that's a distinction without a difference if I ever saw one!"

Chapter Three

The dusty little village of El Cerritos was just a wide spot in the road forty miles southwest of Juarez. It didn't have much to recommend it but it did have two qualities that would attract a man of Ozmundo Rios' ilk; it had a bank and it didn't have a garrison of rurales. The bank was in business primarily to handle the funds of the numerous cattle ranches in the area. It was guarded by a retired former soldier. Local law enforcement was a no longer intimidating, tired old overweight policeman. With this in mind, plus its isolated location in a sparsely populated part of the state, it was an attractive target for dedicated professional lowlifes.

Rios and his men arrived at the village in the early afternoon. They entered the cantina in groups of two's and three's some minutes apart. He sat drinking where he could watch the bank across the street. Finally an older man with a dark suit walked out and locked the door, obviously the bank's owner. Rios nodded to one of his men and without a word being spoken, the outlaw silently left and rode behind the banker to see which house he entered. He returned within a few minutes nodding as he passed Rios' table and resumed drinking in his place at the bar.

Sometime after midnight, the men slipped out of the cantina in the same small groups and quietly rode to the banker's house. They pulled their bandanas over their faces and broke in. The couple was jarred from sleep when the men grabbed the wife yanking her from the bed. She landed in a pile on the floor but before she could scream a toothless bandit jumped astraddle her with a knife at her throat making a preposterous "shushing" sound.

The banker pleaded with the men, "Please don't harm my wife. I'll give you everything I have. Take my money; it's on the table by the bed. Take what you want just don't hurt her, please senor," the terrified man cried looking at Rios since it was obvious he was the leader.

"Oh, we're going to take what we want old man," Rios snapped, "but what we want is not in this house. We want what you have in your bank."

"Just don't hurt my wife! I'll do what you say, just don't hurt her."

Rios said, "Her life is in your hands. Do as I say and she lives; fail, and...you know what happens if you fail. Ride to your bank and put all of the money in a bag and come right back. Don't talk to anyone and don't even let anyone see you or she will die. Remember as you ride to your bank, her life is in your hands. If you have any thoughts of raising an alarm, it will be too bad for her. Now go, and don't bother with your horse, take one of those tied up behind the house. You have a half hour."

The terrified banker did as he was told, but when he returned with the money he found his nude wife dead with her throat cut. It was obvious she had been raped before she was murdered. He dropped to his knees, sickened by the scene, then instantly followed the fate of his wife of thirty years. Rios had left no possible witnesses which was his usual tactic. Regardless of whether or not a victim cooperated, they were always gruesomely dispatched. The dead make poor witnesses.

Stealing anything of value, the gang rode south for about two miles in case they were somehow followed, and then rode out on the range and turned north back towards Juarez.

* * * *

Like the men in the Old Testament who claimed God had ordered them to commit great slaughter of defeated peoples, Jack displayed inverted mental patterns. First he would do an act, and then he would attribute it to God's will. He absolved himself of personal guilt by rationalizing that he was merely meting out God's justice. The Deity always whispered in his ear that they deserved what they got for some past indiscretion. At least, he convinced himself that he had heard God's own voice directing his actions. It was well known that he talked to God, but no-one ever told him that he might be a bit delusional. As word of his successes, at times against great odds, spread it was felt that maybe he was on speaking terms with the Lord after all. Therefore, he saw himself as a warrior angel anointed by the Deity to destroy lawless evil men.

Within three years, he had gathered fifteen more ghosts. Eight men were goaded into a fight while the rest were shot at long range as they tried to cross the river out of Mexico, some were even warned first. That's what the Sharps rifle was for. A horse wading across the river was slow going so the first rider would be dead before the report from the rifle was even heard. From those distances, the bullet would find the man's chest before the sound found his ears.

The rest would invariably turn and flee pell-mell back the direction they had just come from. At first, he found it unseemly to kill a man without giving him the chance to stand and defend himself, but eventually he got past that by reminding himself that these men never gave their victims any semblance of fairness either. It was a bad man's version of "What's good for the goose…"

The Mexican federal constabulary Guardia Rural known as the "rurales," turned a blind-eye to his comings and goings since he was actually aiding them in their law enforcement. The commandant, Colonel Alvaro Silva of the Juarez garrison even sent word when someone was in the area he thought Jack may have an interest in. The rurales were a fairly weak and ineffective force against the banditry of the 1870's, so when men like Jack eliminated a wanted bad man, Silva figured it was one less for him to contend with. He never had as many as twenty men under him at any one time and a vast area to patrol, so he was thankful for any help from any quarter.

Silva was the son of a prominent lawyer from Morella, near Mexico City. As a young man in his early twenties, he was found passed out from drunkenness beside the body of a rival for the affections of the daughter of a local dignitary. There was no proof he had killed the man, but it appeared to be so. Owing to his condition the night before, he was unsure himself so his father used his connections in the government to have him whisked out of town and assigned to the rurales, where he could blend in and disappear owing to the nature of that organization consisting of former bandits and other undesirables.

He was a likeable sort, and soon his compelling good looks attracted enough female attention that he no longer felt Juarez was the proverbial, "end of the earth" and had come to thrive in his assignment.

Over time, the two men became close friends. It was an odd pairing because Silva had a neat and orderly military mind and Jack's idea of "neat and orderly' was a world free of those he deemed undeserving of God's sunshine. But nonetheless, it was much more than just a functional relationship. It was the kind of brotherly love strong men can develop when they have no brothers of their own. Jack even shared bounties at times for any useful information.

One morning acting on such a tip from Silva, Jack was on the border about seventy miles downriver of El Paso sitting on some large rocks in plain sight when Johnny "Two Dogs" Wilson, a particularly vile and wanton murderer and six companions approached the river from the Mexican side. They stopped when they saw him sitting there in the open with his Sharps across his lap. It was clear that they were surprised at his appearance and were debating among themselves as to what the next move should be when he shouted, "That'll be far enough lads. I wouldn't be steppin' those ponies off into the water unless you're thinkin' of givin' them a wash. You ain't welcome in Texas, except for you Two Dogs. Now you just put your hands up and come on across. Somebody went and put a five hundred dollar bounty on your head and I was thinkin' how much I need the cash. Being stuck out here, I don't always get paid real regular. So keep your hands where I can see them and come on nice and slow."

Wilson looked about at his companions and shouted back, "What are you going to do if I don't come across? You coming over here, you son-of-a-bitch?"

"Lad, you know damn well I'll be comin' to collect your body as soon as it quits floppin' in the dirt. This badge I got says I can shoot your worthless ass if I've a mind. And don't think of runnin', that tree-line behind you is at least a hundred yards and I'll bet you a blind, three-legged dog has a better chance of catchin' a jackrabbit than you've got of makin' it to them trees. Of course you're free to try, I'm supposin'."

"That badge you're wearing is from Texas, and this is Mexico. Your jurisdiction ends at this goddamned river you son-of-a-bitch!"

"My jurisdiction ends when this nasty-assed little ole cannon is out of range…and you ain't nowhere near that far! Besides, that Texas judge who gave me this badge kinda likes me. I make his job easy. He'll just sign my ticket and throw your sorry ass in a hole in the ground!"

Before anything else could be said, a shot rang out. The man at the rear of the group had slowly slid his rifle out of his saddle holster and got off a shot that missed Jack by inches. At the sound, the rest broke for cover in the tree-line and were disappearing by the time Jack had jumped down and started to aim his rifle. He muttered to himself, "Well I'll be a two-headed yellow spider! I guess he made it. It was my fault for runnin' my mouth. Next time I'll just run one through him before I start jawin'."

Jack was not used to failure and fumed for several minutes. He did some mental calculations—they'd ride like hell for a mile or so, and then set an ambush just in case he followed them. The advantage goes to the hunted when the element of surprise is gone and they have time to regroup and lay in wait. He decided to let them sit in the hot sun waiting but he wasn't going to follow. "Let'em bake!" he muttered and rode downstream to see if anything else presented itself.

He rode for about two hours when he decided that he needed some conversation with someone other than himself. He patted his big roan stallion on the neck and said, "I like you lad, but I'm needin' somethin' to ride that smells a lot better than you do," so he crossed into Mexico and headed for his favorite place for that type of riding of a different kind.

Chapter Four

Delia's Cantina sat two miles from the border eighty miles downriver from Juarez, and twelve miles due north of San Tomas. Aside from being twice the size of any other of its kind, it was a typical roadside watering hole for the era. A man could get cheap whiskey and a cheap woman and spend several pleasurable hours for only a moderate amount of money. The women were fairly clean; at least they didn't smell of anything worse than sweat. They were all good at what they did and they were not above separating a sleeping drunk cowboy from his poke. What the women didn't get, the shady card sharks at the tables did. Most men left in the morning broke and hung-over, but grinning.

For the most part, the women were fairly good looking, but none approached the beauty of Delia Hurtado herself. Her curly light brown hair drew attention to the lightest brown eyes imaginable. Her creamy skin color set one's mind to thinking of the finest of porcelain dolls. Her body encouraged more than a few men to talk out loud to themselves. Even the ever present cigarillo she smoked didn't detract from the ultimate in female sexuality she glowed with. She quit plying her trade the night she inherited sole ownership of the cantina when her business partner got himself killed playing poker. When a quick, surprise card count of the deck he was winning with produced six aces, he was shot on the spot. Even for the exceedingly drunk players, six aces raised serious questions as to the game's integrity.

She now satisfied herself with the running of the business. When some newcomer would ask her price, she would always shout that he couldn't afford her unless he owned a mine somewhere. Everyone would laugh even though she said it at least twenty times a night. Since no mine owner ever crossed her threshold, it was never learned what that price might actually be.

The usual clientele was a rough combination of outlaws, gunfighters, bounty hunters and those with something to hide. An impossibly obese woman with an angelic face and voice known only as Estella, played guitar and sang plaintive love songs. There were the ubiquitous peons as well looking to pry loose a peso or two doing whatever task they could dredge up.

Delia didn't much interfere with the goings on except for out and out armed robbery. She also had a couple of seedy looking characters wandering the floor with wooden mallets knocking out angry men calling out other angry men. Even on slow nights, there were usually sixty to seventy men about the place. But try as she may, gun play was a frequent activity and there wasn't much she could do about that. Where bad men drink with half-naked women, trouble attends.

Jack entered through the back door as was his habit. He ordered a steak from the cook and opened the door just a crack to see who was in the big room. Satisfying his curiosity, he sat to wait for his meal. Delia came into the kitchen and seeing him, ran and jumped in his lap. She kissed him long and hard. Finally fighting for breath, he pulled back and said, "Missed me did you lass? If I'd have known this, I'd come more often."

"Liar! I am always this glad to see you, menso! It's just that you must have another woman and don't need to see me so much anymore. Tell me who she is so I can cut her into many tiny pieces!"

"Now who's lying? You ain't jealous so let it be. Besides, you wouldn't hit at a snake even if it was about to bite. So save that fiery 'Mexican wench' silliness for the boyo's in the other room. I know where I stand. You ain't fixin' to be cuttin' on nobody on my account, hell, you'd come closer to cuttin' me!"

She smiled and shook her head, "Menso, I do love you, you must know that. You are the only man I let touch me anymore, but I do get jealous at times, especially when you don't come around. I think that maybe you have found a woman and that hurts me sometimes."

"Delia my sweet, I'd never leave you…you're the perfect woman. You're a hundred times better lookin' than anybody else I've ever seen and you own your own whorehouse!"

She looked hurt over his crude comment, "I know you think what we do here is wicked, but for these women the only other way to survive is making tortillas and babies with some bastard that would beat her for getting fat."

Jack blushed for he was truly embarrassed for his rude comments and uttered, "Christ on the cross lass, I'm sorry for that 'whorehouse' shit. I was just tryin' to be funny. I'm the last person on earth that would disparage how another made a livin', considering what I do. Forgive me?"

She started laughing, "The look on your face is prefect! I have always wondered what it would take to make you lose some of that famous Irish arrogance. I might have known it would take something out of your own mouth to humble you. Of course I forgive you menso, how long are you staying this time?"

"At least for the night, I doubt if you'll still be talkin' to me by the mornin'…as usual," he grinned. "Now if you don't mind, I need a bath."

"Yes you do—and I would never mind that menso!"

Later after intense lovemaking, Jack lay beside her and softly and lightly scratched Delia's entire body with his fingernails from her inner thighs to the hollow of her neck. She had long since taught him that she enjoyed "after-play" nearly as much as "foreplay" and the act itself. It kept the pleasure alive as long as possible. He had discovered the most important lesson a man could learn—if he satisfied her, she would see to it that he was satisfied in turn.

As he lazily traced circles on her breasts outlining her nipples, he smiled and said, "Damn lass, I'll be a two-headed yellow spider if I don't think that was the best I ever had." With that, he kissed each breast.

She grinned mischievously and playfully grabbed his genitals and said, "That's because you're thinking with this, and this has a short memory, menso. The next time will also be the best, and then the time after that will be the best as well. This little cabrone is very forgetful, that is its nature."

He grinned and teased, "Hell lass, maybe you're right. I suppose I could always find out for myself by takin' one of the other girls next time. Like Erlinda I'm supposin'. I kinda like the way she's put together."

She impishly squeezed what she held in her hands and said, "If you do, you won't have this to use!"

They both laughed and made love again before they slept.

Sometime shortly after midnight, he awoke from a terrible dream. He was drenched in sweat and shook his head several times to rid himself of the frightening images. The face of a woman from his past was as real in his dream as it ever was in life. In his dream, Margarita Salcido was floundering in a deep and fast moving river but he could not reach her. She was drowning and he was helpless to do anything about it. He was frustrated because as he swam towards her, the current kept pulling her just out of reach. The look of terror in her eyes turned to disgust at his ineptness and finally to anger that he was letting her die, but he could do nothing, save watch her scream "Jack!" It was her screams that sounded as if they were in the room that woke him.

Delia was still sleeping and had not noticed his movements. He sat on the side of the bed for several minutes. The dream was so real to him, his hands still shook. He was one that believed in omens, so there was some reason for the dream. He sensed the message was she was in danger and he must go to see about it. He would go to the Salcido ranch and check things out for himself. He awakened Delia and lied to her about going back to El Paso for some just remembered reason and promised to not stay away so long in the future. She called him a liar and rolled back over. He patted her perfectly round rump, and said goodbye.

As he rode the twelve miles to San Tomas, his mind went back to 1868 when he had met the family. They were under the guns of a half dozen bandits when he chased them away. He had sat out the Civil War in San Tomas refusing to take sides, and afterwards he frequently made trips back. On that day, he was just aimlessly wandering around the countryside as young single men do when he ran across the holdup. He killed two of the bandits and the others fled. The family was grateful and invited him to spend some time on their ranch.

He enjoyed being in a family atmosphere for the first time in years and over time, his frequent visits resulted in his falling in love with the eldest daughter, Margarita. The romance ended when he left to keep her from being exposed to the dangers of his lifestyle. He had had a gunfight while in her presence and decided it was too dangerous for her to be anywhere around him. It was a difficult thing to do, but he would never consider giving up the way of the gun, therefore leaving her was the only option.

He turned in the gate and rode up to the main house of the hacienda. There was a small crowd in the great room. None of them were known to him except Tony and Nettie, Margarita's parents. They were both sobbing in obvious grief. He walked up to them and spoke, "What is the matter my friend? What happened?"

Nettie was near collapse and unable to speak, but Tony whispered, "It's Margarita. She was murdered tonight. Her and her husband also."

His knees nearly buckled. Margarita and her husband murdered? He didn't know she was married, but it had been five years since he had seen her. Life goes on, but now her life has been ended. He could barely speak, "How?"

Tony braced himself as well as he could and began, "Sometime after midnight, armed men broke into their house in San Tomas and demanded all of the money in Rodrigo's bank for the safe release of Margarita."

Jack interrupted, "Rodrigo's bank? Was that her husband?"

"Yes. Three years ago, she met and married Rodrigo Delgado. His family owns a large bank in Chihuahua and a small one in San Tomas. These men demanded that he bring all of the money in the safe and they would let her go. But when he returned home, they had ravaged her and put a bullet in her brain. They shot him too, but he lived for an hour. They thought he was dead, so they talked freely and he learned who they were. The doctor who tried to save his life said Rodrigo told him this before he died."

Jack demanded, "Who was the som-bitch? And where can I find him?"

"His name is Ozmundo Rios, and he is usually around the border near Juarez. Do you know him? You are there too, no?"

"Yes I'm on the border, but I stay on the Texas side sometimes up to a couple hundred miles downriver, but I won't be now by God! I'll be on his ass until I put one in his head. He's goin' to regret that his father ever mounted his mother…count on it!"

Tony pointed to a tall good looking man in a well tailored uniform, "Do see that man? He is Captain Garza of the police in San Tomas. He is in charge of the investigation. He can tell you more than I can."

Jack walked up to the captain and introduced himself. The captain said, "Mucho gusto senor. Senor Salcido has spoken of you. It is indeed my pleasure." With that he extended his hand.

Jack, impatient with chit-chat, pressed on, "Tony tells me you can give me some information on this mongrel, Ozmundo Rios."

"He is a bad man who, so far, has never been close to being caught. He is suspected in at least a dozen murders, maybe more, but there are never any witnesses to say for sure. He must have a hideout somewhere south of Juarez, possibly towards Casas

Grande for he is often seen there. He rides with six other men, one of which is the wanted murderer Johnny Wilson of Texas. Have you heard of him?"

"Two Dogs!? Well I'll be goddamned! Does this Rios bird dress in all black with a black sombrero and ride a big white stud?"

"Then you have seen him?" the captain asked.

"You're goddamned right I've seen him! I had the lot of them under my gun yesterday but they got away!"

"That does not sound like the Jack Rose they tell stories about."

"I was too busy spoofin' with Wilson tryin' to scare the hell out of him. If I'd have known they would then ride this way, I'd have hung the lot of them with their own guts, by God!"

He instantly thought of his dream and reasoned, "No wonder I couldn't save her, I'm the som-bitch that got her killed." He was devastated that his own arrogance had cost her, her life. He had been sitting on the rocks showing off when he should have been down in them blowing giant holes in the bastards instead. He knew then why he had had the dream at the same time she was dying—God was angry with him for being a failure after he had been presented with a golden opportunity to destroy these evil men. God was making it known that his seeking petty personal pleasures had costs.

A Cheyenne friend once said that God had created "protectors" to stand between the men who were predators and the defenseless who were the preyed upon. The only redemption for a failed protector was in becoming an "avenger". He was at once confident he would not fail again. He vowed to show these men the wrath of God's avenger!

He walked outside onto the veranda to catch his breath. He looked towards the heavens and promised God that he was truly repentant and begged to be allowed to find those vermin. In return, he promised to not use His name in vain ever again. As he stood there a voice from behind made him jump, "Jack?"

He whirled around and almost lost all power of speech. There before him in the moonlight was his once beloved Margarita. Unable to move or speak, he remained frozen where he was. He had just been told she was dead, but there she stood beckoning him. It must be her ghost, what else could it be? Her spirit, or whatever it was, was so real he swore he could smell her perfume.

The voice said again, "Jack…" He thought he was losing his mind until the voice continued, "It's me, Carolina. Don't you recognize me?"

"Of course I recognize you," he lied. He was shaken at the likeness with her sister as he continued, "I'm sorry…it's just that you took my breath away. Damn lass, you've fetched up well. You ain't no longer the little pig-tailed pest I remember. You must be nearly…what…sixteen by now? I know you shouldn't tell a woman she has grown, but I'll be a two-headed yellow spider if I know what to say!"

"I turned eighteen last month, but I think you did just fine. I've never had a compliment quite like it."

"Well come here and let me get a better look at you." He put his arms around her and hugged her tightly and kissed her cheeks. He held a woman and not the awkward adolescent he once knew. He then remembered Margarita and was sad again. He said after a slight pause, "I'm so sorry for your family. I can't imagine what you are going through. I've never had anyone I care about die before and don't exactly know what to do. But I am here to do what I can for the family before I hunt down that god…" he caught himself when he remembered his vow. "Excuse me. I'm tryin' to watch my language, but I'm going to hunt down Ozmundo Rios and end his days in the most painful manner I can come up with…I promise."

"Jack, I know my mother and father are so glad you are here. They have missed you, and I have too for that matter. Mother even said when we heard the news that if you had only been here, this would not have happened. She loved Rodrigo, but she had really wanted you for a son-in-law."

She did not mean it the way he took it. She had made a simple statement of fact, but in his guilt enveloped mind, it was further condemnation. This confirmed for him that his carelessness had been the cause of her death. Even this sweet child's mother knew that his absence had, in fact put her on a course of inevitable destruction. Worse yet, his arrogance permitted her killers to escape his guns and put Margarita in front of theirs. He was confused that if God had demanded him to be responsible for her fate, why was he allowed to leave her in the first place? Why was he not given a sign at the time?

Then at that particular moment, he suddenly felt compelled to talk to someone about what was torturing his soul. He was reluctant to confide in Tony or Nettie, but for some reason he felt he could share his burden with Carolina. He asked her to sit on the steps of the veranda and listen quietly until he had finished. He had never before opened up to a living human being and he felt that if he was interrupted at any point, he would probably not summon the strength to continue.

For the next several minutes he told her everything he was wrestling with; his part in Margarita's ultimate destruction by both deserting her, leaving her unprotected and then failing her again by letting her killers escape condemning her to the mercies of merciless men. He even told of the prophetic dream, but he politely left out where he was when it came to him. He finally questioned how God could have gotten it so wrong by destroying a precious and innocent woman instead of him for whatever grudge the Almighty might be harboring.

She was deeply touched that the Jack Rose of her youth, who was the knight in shining armor and the destroyer of evil men, was capable of the depths of emotion he now displayed. She reached out and took his hand in hers and said softly, "God didn't get it wrong. You are mortal and cannot foresee what evil men may possibly do. He doesn't test us by taking the lives of others. We grieve for the loss of someone's earthly presence, but God is more concerned with gathering their souls about Him for eternity. Earthly existence is over quickly but heavenly grace is forever. You should not feel guilt for Margarita's murder. Even if you had stayed and married her, something else could have happened at any time. An accident that you had no control over could have befallen her, would you blame yourself for that? Of course not; evil men have free will and choose to do evil things and you'll never be able to foresee what they may plan to do."

He reflected on what she had just said and blurted out unguardedly, "I love you..." He quickly caught himself and tried to save it, "You know what I mean...I love you for what you're tryin' to do...that's all I meant," he blushed.

She reached over and kissed his forehead and said, "And I love you, but I'm not going to babble some feeble attempt at mitigation, I simply love you; I always have, now good night." She went into the house which had emptied of the people who had been there earlier to give solace to the family, and to bed.

He was confounded at his emotions and couldn't decide which was more powerful, his guilt or his enchantment by her last utterance. He was still sitting on the steps with his mind in a jumble when Tony stepped out and said that he should use the guestroom at the head of the stairs. He declined saying he was used to sleeping outside and was just fine on the veranda. Tony nodded and promised they would talk in the morning and retired.

Jack pushed two chairs together and tried to sleep, but his mind would not slow down enough for that to happen. All he managed was hours of random remembrances of Margarita and quite a few images bouncing around in his head of her little sister as well.

Just after first light, Tony brought two cups of coffee and rejoined him on the veranda. He summoned the courage to tell the man of his guilt. He was not surprised that Tony took the news exactly as his daughter had. Being of the same blood and environment, they would naturally think alike. The words were a little different, but the message was exactly the same—Jack could not see the future so he could not be responsible for any of the actions of others. To assume such responsibility upon oneself was arrogance and an insult to God.

Jack looked Tony in the eye and said, "I've always respected you as a good and wise man, but you're as wrong as hell in this. God is tryin' to get my attention. How else can you explain my idiocy ended up costin' her life? And why else would He allow those murderin' bastards to escape my guns by makin' me act so foolish by showin' off tryin' to scare the hell out of them first before I sent them to meet Him personally? No Tony, God's disappointed in me and is screamin' in my ear what a sorry som-bitch I am!"

"No my son, that is merely your desire to make yourself more important in Margarita's destiny than you actually were. When you left, that was a noble act and you were to be commended for such selflessness. It is God's will that she is dead, not your failure. To claim otherwise is to usurp the power of God."

"Well all of that may be true, but He's changed his mind and is now shoutin' at me to get off my ass and find those bastards and introduce them to Satan! That's what I'm goin' to do…I'll be back when I've finished."

Tony asked if he was not staying for the funeral which he answered that he had Rios' funeral to plan for instead. He begged that if he stayed, the trail may grow cold. With that, he put his badge in his pocket and rode north and west towards Juarez intent on gathering of seven more ghosts…that or becoming one himself trying.

Chapter Five

Three days later, Wilson and two of Rios' men burst into Carlos' Cantina forty miles southeast of Juarez. It was obvious that they were agitated as they sat at a corner table furthest from the door. They threw down shot after shot of tequila as they watched the door carefully. Their nervousness was apparent even among a room full of nervous men. They reached for their guns when the door would open and relax only after they saw that the man who terrified them was not the man who entered.

One of the men, a particularly ugly man with no hair or front teeth who went by the name of Baldy, finally broke the silence, "If that devil, Rose was coming for us, wouldn't we have seen him by now?"

The other man with a vicious scar on his left cheek that started at an eye patch and ended at his chin called Paco, offered, "I have never heard of him coming this far south. We're nearly sixty miles from his part of the border."

Wilson glared at both men and snorted, "You're dumber than horse piss! If that son-of-a-bitch got the scent of a man in his nostrils, he'd ride all the way to Panama! Just keep watching the door! He's coming, I feel it! He ain't going to let us off without so much as a 'kiss my ass!' You took a shot at him, you reckon he'll forgive that?" looking at Paco.

Paco interjected, "He won't come here. The army won't allow him that much freedom to move where he wants. They will stop him before he gets this far."

Wilson snarled, "Who, those sons-of-bitches? Hell, they'd piss themselves at the first sight of that bastard! Just stay alert and don't get drunk!"

Wilson and his two companions were still sitting at the same table towards midnight when the door swung open and their worst fears glared back at them. Jack stood in the open door with nothing but a few feet of space between them and the infernal regions. He cast a careful eye on the few customers still there to see if any were known to him or if any had unpleasant ideas and then said in a slow and deliberate voice, "Don't even blink you som-bitch! You ain't the one I'm lookin' for this day. Tell me where Rios is and you keep breathin' if not, you won't be here for the end of this conversation!"

The men had been drinking for several hours and had long since passed the point where alcohol fueled machismo defeats intelligence and Wilson jumped up tossing the table in front of him and shouted, "You bastard!" as he reached for his weapon. His gun had not cleared leather when the first bullet ripped its way through his chest. The second hit a dead man falling to the floor. The other two men were waving their hands wildly in the air making sure that Jack saw they were no threat.

He turned his attention to the two men begging for their lives. Baldy was terrified and standing in a pool of his own urine so Jack started with him. "I suppose you heard the question that dead idiot wasn't bright enough to answer?"

"I don't know, I swear it! We split up two days ago and he said he would catch up later! I swear it! I don't know where he is for Christ's sake!" he said on the verge of tears.

Jack looked at Paco and continued, "I know you. You're the bastard that took a shot at me. You want to try it again? Well do ya? It ain't so easy with a man standin' close enough to smell the sweat, now is it? Here's the last chance you'll ever be gettin'!" After about a five second wait, he pulled the trigger blowing the man's navel out through the back of his shirt. He shouted over his shoulder to the roomful of witnesses, "I say this pile of dog-shit went for his gun—anyone see it different?"

The few men with the nerve to reply all agreed with Jack's version. He had had no doubt of what the results of his straw poll would be, and he turned back to Baldy. He dropped down to his knees and continued begging for his life. Jack told him to find saddle leather and tell Rios what his future looked like. He was out the door before Jack had finished his sentence.

He turned to the bartender and asked if he had seen the whole thing. He said yes so Jack tossed him a small note book and pencil and told him to write what he had witnessed. The man said that he could not write in English only Spanish. Jack said that was better since the note was for the Mexican judge in Juarez if he decided to investigate. He then told the bartender that he could claim Wilson's reward himself for all he cared. He nodded to a stunned Carlos and left.

Two nights later sitting in the same cantina, Rios heard the story when Baldy caught up to him. He had been hiding for fear that Jack would change his mind and hunt him down after all. After what he had witnessed, he was terrified of that possibility. He had two days and nights to ponder actually looking for Rios to give him the message, or blind flight as far away from the man as possible. Being a hopeless coward with no strivings for independence, he reluctantly came back to the cantina and his natural position in the shadows of a strong man.

According to his story, Jack gave no warning. He just opened fire as he entered, in effect, murdering Wilson and Paco as they sat innocently playing cards. In his version, it was out and out unprovoked murder.

The bartender shouted that that was not true. During the course of each evening, he handled much meaner individuals than Baldy ever was. The caliber of the clientele was such that a wrong look could have consequences. He was a former gunman himself and held no fear of such men. He told of Jack's offer for Wilson to live if he told where Rios was and what followed after that. He also added that Jack had sent a message with this "mongrel" that Rios was next which is why he figured it took so long for Baldy to find him in the very spot he had fled from. He must have been afraid to be anywhere near Rios if Jack was still in the area. None the less, Baldy begged that he had earnestly looked for Rios to give warning.

He dismissed all with a wave of his hand and asked, "Why does this gringo bastard want a fight with me? I have heard of him, but the other day at the crossing was the first time I ever saw him. I have not done anything on his side of the border. What is wrong with this cabrone?"

Rios got tired of taxing his brain and ordered another bottle. What he needed was more drinking and less thinking and that he did with great gusto for the next several hours. By midnight he was roaring drunk when he saw a pretty little blond whore sitting on the lap of an attentive cowboy. He asked the bartender her name and was surprised when he was told "Beverly Rose." He came to a tequila-soaked conclusion and acted on it.

As he walked towards her, she stood up frightened by his reputation. He smiled as he punched her viciously in the stomach. Fighting for breath, she fainted which was a mercy for what happened next. Rios kicked and stomped her several times screaming for her to tell her bastard brother that this was what awaited him. The cowboy on whose lap she had been sitting jumped up in a feeble attempt at chivalry. He was killed for his trouble by one of Rios' men. The shot set off a volley of reflexive gunfire from every direction. Three men lay dead, one of which was a Rios man. He and what was left of his gang left in a hurry heading south.

Colonel Silva from the Juarez garrison had heard of the shootout, so he and several of his men walked into Carlos' to investigate. He learned from the bartender the facts behind Wilson's death and the beating Beverly Rose received at the hands of Rios. The girl was confined to her bed in bad shape. One of the women took him to see her where he interviewed her as much as she could stand. He was appalled at the terrible shape she was in. Her face was terribly bruised and her eyes were swollen nearly shut. He was also told there had been blood in her urine and spittle. She could tell him little of the beating since she was unconscious through most of it. Witnesses had said that Rios kept yelling that it was "for her brother," but she told the colonel that she had no idea what that meant. She answered his question with her full name, Beverly Rose Fahey. Silva knew instantly it was a case of mistaken identity when Rios had taken her middle name for her last. The girl was very lucky to still be alive. He assured her that he would arrest Rios soon and she was safe for now. He then advised Carlos to have someone stand guard in case Rios came back. He added that whoever that was should shoot first by all means. There would be no questions afterwards on the colonel's part.

Silva took his leave and rode back to headquarters. On the trip back, he pondered his next move. He could spend time and search for Rios over the widespread area he was known to ride, or he could look for Jack since the bartender had told of the threat he had issued that day for Rios' man to deliver. He decided that since Jack had some reason to want Rios already, he would merely add fuel to the fire by telling him of the girl's beating and let him handle it from there. That would be best for all concerned, after all Jack was the professional in these matters.

He raised his hand for the column to halt. He sent several men to comb the Mexican side of the river and others to ride checking the villages on the main road towards San Tomas. Between the two units, surely one would find him. He stressed to his men that their job was to relay the message and nothing more and if they found Rios first, to merely track him and not engage, unless fired upon.

He continued his trip feeling that he had done the best thing for him and his men. Even though most of them were men with hard pasts, none of them were experienced enough to take on such a killer of Rios' caliber. He laughed as he thought to himself that he wouldn't give a dead cat for Rios' future. "He's pissed off the wrong man!"

His efforts were wasted as he discovered upon entering the garrison compound. Jack's big roan was tied to the post in front of Silva's office. He found the Irishman sitting behind his desk and said, "If you're looking for the tequila, it's in the bottom left drawer."

"I know that jefe, I was looking for the glasses" Jack said putting the bottle on top of the desk.

"Since when did brothers need glasses? Are you suddenly too good to drink after me?" he laughed as he took a long pull from the bottle.

Taking his drink in turn, he said, "Al, I need your help to find a man that is anxious to see what hell looks like!"

"Rios?"

"How did you know? Oh, I guess you've heard about Wilson and that other mongrel."

"I stopped at Carlos' and heard of the threat you sent to Rios and the beating he gave to one of the girls...a Beverly Rose Fahey...he damn near killed her thinking she was your sister because of the 'Rose' in her name. As he stomped her, he kept cussing you." He was eager to inflame the situation further to watch Jack's reaction.

Jack then told of Margarita's murder and the circumstances surrounding it. Silva, in turn, told of the incident at El Cerritos and how the similarities were too great to ignore.

Jack said, "I'll be two-headed yellow spider if I don't kill that som-bitch one second after I lay eyes on him! Have you got any idea where that bastard is now?"

"No, but I have two patrols out now with orders to follow him if they find him."

"Good lad. I'll be back tomorrow to see what you've found. I've got to go to El Paso and find that skin-flint judge. I need some money since my credit is gettin' thin. I owe every café and cantina on both sides of the border for fifty miles god..." he stopped short of finishing. He was trying.

They shook hands and Jack headed for the bridge at the border crossing. Later he walked into Judge Shafer's office. The judge looked up from his desk and said, "Well as I live and breathe. How are you my boy?"

"I'd be a hell of a lot better if I had some money. I ain't been paid in three months."

The judge smiled and said, "Actually it has been only one. I saw the records just this morning."

"I admit that I ain't the smartest man with a hat, but I can count to three! That's what you owe me, plus the five hundred dollar bounty on Charlie Elmore. I turned in that ticket last month if you remember."

"I remember, but I also remember having to give it to a very irate saloon owner from Nogales who said you shot up his place and broke his fancy mirror behind the bar."

"Nogales? I ain't never been that far west! He's lyin'."

"That might be, but he showed up with a signed court order from a judge claiming damages. It looked authentic to me, what choice did I have? Federal court judges tend to honor the decrees of other judges. It works out well that way, besides they can arrest you for ignoring one of their writs. I couldn't have that; how would it look having my deputy arrested for shooting a goddamned mirror? Were you drunk and you scared the shit out of yourself?"

37

Jack looked the judge directly in the eye. After a few seconds, he decided the man was lying but how could he prove it? If the judge had said that a war party of Apaches had stolen it, he would have some sort of document signed by Geronimo himself to back his play. He snorted, "Well what about my three months pay?"

The judge grinned sensing that he had Jack at last and said, "Well let's see...you say three and I say one...how about us splitting the difference and say two?" He slid a sealed envelope across the desk with the requisite two month's pay inside. He had it ready all along.

"Why you connivin' old som..." he caught himself, because he was talking to a judge after all, "You had this planned! You knew how much you could get away with. And that shit about a bar owner in Nogales...when I leave here I'm goin' to go and look him up, if he even exists!"

"Now son, I wouldn't do that if I was you. Judges don't necessarily like folks callin' them liars. You can do what you want, but I'd think about it long and hard." He was lying and worse, he knew that Jack knew it too, but he was in a hole and had to keep digging.

"That lyin' som-bitch in Nogales is lucky that I've got important doin's right now and ain't got the time to go and set him straight. There's a no-account scum in Mexico that needs killin' bad. I have to go and see about him, but I'll be back."

"Jack, before you go, think about this...I can't protect you down there if you get in a tight. If they get a new regime with new men in power, it could go bad for you, so be very careful."

Jack thought it nice that the judge cared enough to warn him to be careful. But after about a minute, he decided the short, fat, balding old thief was probably just pretending to care. He was as full of shit as a Christmas goose, but you had to like him.

Chapter Six

Jack was hidden in some rocks watching the three riders who approached from a great distance. One wore black and rode a white horse so he figured it was Rios. He slowly raised the Sharps to his shoulder and started to focus the sights when he was startled by a decidedly female voice that pleaded, "Please don't shoot my father senor!"

He rolled over and shaded his eyes from the sun and saw a barefooted peasant girl he guessed to be about twenty years of age with a frightened look on her face. He bellowed, "Christ on the cross lass! Don't go sneakin' around a man doin' his job. It ain't fittin' and besides, you could get yourself shot."

"I saw you from my house," she pointed to a sad small frame house in the distance, "and watched as you hid in the rocks. When I saw that it was El Condor, I was afraid but I had to see who was to be killed."

Jack asked, "El Condor? Who the happy hell is 'El Condor?'"

"You are senor. People say that if they see you near, there will soon be a body to be found. When I saw that it was my father that you aimed at, I became afraid. That is why I begged you not to kill him senor."

He snarled, "Well that lucky man probably owes you his life. What is your name, lass?"

"Anna Garcia, senor, and that is my father Reyes," she waved as the older man rode up.

Reyes recognized Jack and was surprised when Anna explained that she had seen him climbing around the rocks taking aim at him.

He looked at Jack with a puzzled look and asked, "Why was I the target senor? I have offended no one. I am a simple farmer with these three children, Anna, Chato, and Pedro," he said as he pointed to the two teenaged riders with him.

"Well senor Garcia, it was a case of mistaken identity as your lovely daughter was pointin' out when you rode up. I'm beggin' your pardon, but I probably wouldn't have been firin' before I got a good look. I'd have seen you weren't Rios, so you probably wouldn't have been shot...maybe...I'm supposin'," he grinned.

"The man you seek is Ozmundo Rios?"

"Do you know him?"

"Si senor, he is one of many bandits that terrorize the people by stealing whatever they wish. We can do nothing to stop them."

"Senor Garcia, you won't have to be worrin' about that particular som-bitch for very much longer. I'll be sendin' him through hell's front door the instant I see him!"

Reyes pointed at his house and asked, "Senor Rose, will you accept the hospitality of a poor farmer?"

Jack smiled, "I'd be obliged, but how the happy hell did you know who I was? I almost never come to these parts."

Anna spoke up, "I told you senor; everyone knows who El Condor is. He is the great Jack Rose of Texas."

Jack said, "I ain't no goddamned vulture!" then he laughed and added, "Well maybe I am after all. I know Senor Saddle Scum is goin' to think so anyway."

They walked to the house and Anna served them cool water from the well. She sat on a large rock and studied the face of this famous and dangerous man. She had never been in the presence of one quite like him. His red hair and freckles distinguished him from anyone she had even seen. He was handsome enough she thought, but not with the slick, polished look of the elite grandees. He was handsome in a rugged, manly way.

When she recognized him as the one who was setting up a possible ambush, she was compelled to run and see who was in his sights. She had never personally witnessed a person being killed and her curiosity was too great to resist. Her heart had pounded with anticipation at what, seemly, was about to happen. But her realization that it was her father who was about to be shot caused near panic in her. Now an hour or so later, she was beginning to like this strange man. He evidently was attracted to her as well by the way he continually smiled at her and seemingly watched her every move. She was surprised at herself for not being uncomfortable at his attention, but in fact she was beginning to enjoy his apparent interest. She had never had a man look at her quite like this and she thought it nice.

He kept looking at the girl and he decided that she was very pretty. She was no Delia, but nobody was. He enjoyed the way she talked and the way she moved. He was becoming quite taken with her but his musings were interrupted when he saw in the distance a rider approaching in great haste. It was a rurale waving his hand back and forth, yelling to get his attention. He reined his horse to a stop and blurted breathlessly, "Senor Rose, Colonel Silva wishes for you come quickly. He has Ozmundo Rios trapped in a box canyon some few miles from here. He begs for you to come before he is forced to shoot Rios himself."

Jack leapt to his feet and bounded to his horse. As he mounted he said, "Senor Garcia, you're about to have one less bandit bitin' you on the ass, I'm thinkin'." He received an open invitation and promised to return soon.

They rode for the canyon where Rios was holed up. When they arrived, Silva explained a patrol had chased the bandit into a box canyon and sealed it off. When he was informed, he immediately sent some men to fan out and search for Jack. The remaining men were under orders to hold their positions and not fire unless the bandits tried to escape.

He crammed a fistful of cartridges for his Sharps in his pocket and asked Silva, "How many are up there?"

"Four total, counting Rios."

"Hell, you could have shot the other three, you know! I swear I wouldn't have been too riled," he laughed.

"We couldn't. They are out of range; too far up in there."

Jack grinned, "Someday I'll teach you the art of doin' this silliness. Fifteen against four should have been over in two minutes and you especially should never have let them take cover on the high ground on top of that."

"Well, show us how it's done, mi general!" he snorted.

Jack, continuing the smart-aleck banter added, "Just hide and watch hermano, just hide and watch."

He turned and ran to the giant rocks that formed the canyon. He started to weave his way up and though them until he was out of sight.

A few minutes later, he looked down into a bowl-like clearing in the rocks. He saw Rios leaning against a large boulder, aimed his rifle and the unmistakable report from the Sharps announced its presence taking the bandit's manhood with the first shot. Instantly the voices of lesser weapons joined the deadly chorus. Amid the incessant roil of pistol and rifle fire, would be the intermittent bark of the Sharps. While Rios lay screaming on the ground, Baldy's head exploded from a shot to the temple and the others died behind the rocks they hid among. Soon, all sound ceased.

Several minutes later, Jack emerged. Silva had not been overly concerned for Jack's safety because the last sound had been that of the Sharps, so his ordered military mind knew his friend was alive for the last shot. He thought for a moment and said to Jack, "By the way, there were only three other men besides Rios yet we heard at least eight or nine shots from your rifle. Don't tell me you are getting so old that you can no longer shoot straight?"

"Hell no! I was merely tryin' to figure the right angle to bounce a bullet off the rocks in behind them's all. I finally did it, and the dumb-asses died where they hid. Rios quit early not havin' balls and such any longer, so I saved finishin' him for last. When he asked me why I was hunting him, you should have seen the look on his face when I said it was because of Margarita. The pig had no idea who I was talkin' about! So I let his sorry ass bleed to death in what I'd assume was great pain. The important thing is that at this very minute, he's got Satan gnawin' on his sorry ass."

As he rode for the Salcido ranch to give the news, he made a brief stop at the Garcia farm to do the same, but mainly to see the pretty little peasant girl again. There was something captivating about the adorably sexy urchin.

Chapter Seven

He made his way back to the Salcido ranch to tell of Rios' demise. The family was greatly relieved that the ordeal was over and he was unharmed. At Nettie's insistence, they had lit candles at the church for his safe return. Tony felt Jack's skill and savagery would see him through, but as in all things, he bowed to his wife's wishes. So with great relief and thanks to God, they welcomed him and listened to the story.

In the typical fashion of young men, Ricardo and Roberto, the fifteen year old twins pressed for details, the gorier the better. Also, in typical fashion for Jack, he gladly obliged and regaled them with a shot by shot recounting of the battle beginning with the first removing Rios' "particular's" to exploding Baldy's head all over the rocks and ending with Rios' final agony.

Nettie was a little taken aback by the depth of detail thinking it was a little too much for her sensibilities, but what alarmed her the most during the story was her daughter's unmistakable grinning throughout. Carolina absolutely loved every second of it which worried her greatly. Her daughter had always acted more like a boy than a girl and now her reactions to the story frightened her.

She asked Carolina to join her in the kitchen for a minute, and when they were alone she began, "Mija, your attitude frightens me. That look on your face tells me you are not finished with your fascination with guns and bad men."

"Mother, Rios' death makes me very glad for Margarita, but sad that it was not my bullet in his head, my hatred was such. I have never had men look at me like they do for Jack. The respect in their eyes almost takes your breath away and I want that for me. I don't want people to say 'there goes Carolina, what a nice woman she is' I want them to say 'there goes Carolina, she is quite a woman!' Do you see the difference?"

"What are you saying?"

"I'm saying that I intend to go back to the border with him when he returns to his work. He has much to teach me and I have much to learn."

"Carolina! Jack could not have told you that."

"Well, no not really. In fact if you want to see him scream just watch when I tell him. I'm sure you will hear every cuss word that redheaded Irishman knows."

Nettie sat down in a chair suddenly feeling as though the breath had been wrung out of her. The words she was hearing could not possibly be true. Her daughter was no longer content with just being independent and self-assured in a world controlled by men; she now wanted to live like one.

She couldn't blame Jack for this nonsense for he has always been the same with no pretenses. She knew he hadn't encouraged Carolina with this folly, in fact she agreed with her daughter that he will more than likely explode when given the news. If he had tried to spare Margarita from this life, he surely would not encourage Carolina to embrace it. She stood back up and as they re-entered the room with the men she prayed for his eruption.

The conversation finally pointed in the direction Carolina wanted when she made her announcement. Tony smiled weakly and said, "My child, I have watched you everyday of your life, child and woman, and have feared something like this would eventually find its way into your head. Even as a child, you never chose to do things as the other girls. The happiest you had ever been was when Jack taught you to handle guns." He nodded to Jack and continued, "I am not blaming you mijo, it was something she wanted to do, and at the time I myself thought it was a good idea. It is not that I believe she wants to be a man, but she has always demanded to be respected as one. So I do not think the idea is disgraceful, but I do think it is dangerous. So I must demand 'patria potesta' and forbid it. I must be a father this once."

Jack asked Tony, "Patria potesta? What is that?"

"That is the legal right of a father to control the property and life of unmarried children. And in this case, I do exercise that right. I must insist."

Carolina snapped, "I'll be damned! I'll just marry Jack and be done with your precious rights! As a married woman, I will no longer be considered a child."

A startled Jack stammered, "I'll bet a pissed-off Bantam Rooster that this silliness will never be happenin'. First off, if we ever get married you'll have to ask a lot nicer than that. And second, I don't have the power to make you a deputy's deputy if there is even such a thing. And third, it ain't fittin', I've had my say! Oh yeah, fourth, I'm thinkin' of quitin' this mess anyway. I've had enough doin's with lowlife pigs. I was thinkin' of askin' your daddy for a job chasin' horses instead of chasin' men by god! Now I've had my say!"

"Jackie, my son," (he was the only one other than O'Brian and Silva to call him by that name) "you can stay here as long as you wish. This family owes you a debt we can never repay. If you decide to come to work here, you will be welcome."

"I'm thinkin' about it, I swear I am. A man needs somethin' more in life than sleepin' at the river swattin' flies and swattin' saddle scum as well, I'm thinkin'."

Carolina did not speak to him for the rest of his visit, but she had no intention of letting it end where it was. She would make the big lug accept her as she was and teach her to face armed dangerous men whether he knew it or not. She also thought about her snap proposal of marriage. She had been angry at her father and had blurted it out. However she had loved him since childhood, so the idea was serious even if the manner was not. At that moment, she decided to set her sights on him in earnest and make him think it was his idea to boot. Of that she had no doubt she would be successful. She already knew he thought she was beautiful, he had said as much, so she began to hatch a plan to make him think she was compellingly desirable as well.

Tony told him he would always be welcome at the ranch and to let him know what he finally decided. They made small talk for a couple of hours before Jack took his leave.

As he rode away, he let his mind wander from Carolina to Delia, and Anna worked her way into his increasingly jumbled mind as well. Even though he cared a lot for Delia, he had not had strong feelings for a woman since he had left Margarita. For the first time in his life, his thoughts were of more than one woman at the same time. He decided that it was a pleasant experience to have three women on his mind. He had absolutely no idea what he was going to do about it, but it was nice. Maybe God had gotten over His snit after all.

His thoughts were interrupted when he ran across three men starting across the river. He stopped them by saying, "That's far enough lads. Who are you and what's your business in Texas?"

They kept wading on and one shouted, "What's it to you?"

"I merely asked you a civilized question but I'll bet you a two-tailed cat you really don't want a response to yours!" he snarled.

The three men stopped and got a lot more amiable in attitude when one of them recognized Jack and whispered to the others. "We're just going home marshal. We're from up Waco way and just seeing what old Mexico was about."

"Relax lad, I could see you were American, but I was just curious to see if there were papers on you. You ain't wanted for nothin' are you?"

"No sir we ain't. Unless they can arrest you for being stupid that is. We got drunk and spent two month's pay at a whore house across the border."

Jack grinned and said, "Ain't no law against bein' silly, I'm supposin'. Been so myself, a time or two." He then waved them on.

Most people act just like they had. They're honest and didn't want any trouble and for the most part the job was boring. The next group did not pass so easily. After they reached shore, they dismounted and fanned out. Jack said "You lads look like there's somethin' gnawin' at you. So let's hear it?"

The man in the center spoke, "My name is Willis Love. You killed my brother at this very crossing while he was still on the Mexican side you bastard!"

"I remember him. That's as close as the smell would let him get. He was Evan Love who the rurales wanted for killin' a man and his wife and rapin' their eight year old daughter, and then he stomped in her head with his boots. So the way I figure it, he deserved to have his head blown clean off, which is what I done! Smack between the eyes by God! You shoulda seen it!"

Love went for his gun and died before he gripped it. Jack immediately looked at the other two. They were both standing with their hands in the air making no move.

He said, "Lads, when I pull a gun on a man, I kill the man that way I ain't havin' to be dealin' with him later. In this case, I ain't goin' to have to be dealin' with you later am I lads?" As they ran for their horses, he added "I thought not."

He tied the body across the man's horse and thought out loud, "There's another ghost I've gathered." By his count, that made thirty-eight. He fussed at himself because it should have been forty, but two were only wounded instead and lived long enough to be hanged later by Shafer.

Since it was getting near dark by this time, he decided to take the body to the nearest sheriff's office the next day to check for bounties and moved several hundred yards into the trees to bed down for the night. He silently hoped he would be able to sleep and not toss and turn with three women's faces haunting him. But then again, he figured if he had to have a head full of images, he could do worse than those.

Part II
The First Act

Note: All references of historical events taken from The Oxford History of Mexico, Michael C. Meyer and William H. Beezley and Wikipedia.

Benito Juarez won the presidency of Mexico by demanding an end to government dominated by a ruling elite, but became just another in the long line of elitists that had gone before. By filling most government positions with political hacks, he showed disrespect for the regular army officers who had supported him in his battle against foreign intervention. Many of these would become his opponents and one in particular would hold a grudge.

When he died in 1872, he was succeeded by vice president Sebastin Lerdo de Tejada whose term was racked by discord and strife throughout Mexico. Despite being constitutionally prohibited from seeking re-election, he announced he was again a candidate for the presidency. Porfirio Diaz, who had once sought to oust Juarez, began a campaign to discredit Tejada by accusing him of corruption and calling for a fair election. When Tejada won, he was removed from office and Diaz proclaimed himself to be president on November 24, 1876. In his Plan of Tuxtepec, he cited as his justification for ousting an elected government was Tejada's disregard of constitutional provisions against reelection making democracy a "cruel joke," and violence against "worthy citizens".

Thus began a period of Mexican history known as "Porfiriato." Thus too, continued the story of a remarkable life.

Chapter Eight

Geoffrey Molina, the personal assistant to the president and a visitor waited patiently in the anteroom for his boss to finish dressing for his first day in office. Eventually a valet appeared and ushered both men into a large and sunny sitting room off of the president's bedroom. Molina smiled as he bowed and said, "Good morning my president. This is Senor Samuel Busterman, the artist you sent for. Senor Busterman, I have the honor to present His Excellency, President Jose de la Cruz Porfirio Diaz." He bowed again and stepped back a respectful distance to appear not to be listening, but close enough where he could.

"Senor Busterman! Welcome my friend. We have long admired your work. Samples of your brilliance hang in the finest museums in Europe and in all of the Americas as well. When the idea came to us, you were the first and only artist that we thought of. It is our hopes that you accept the commission we offer. Molina no doubt has told you, we plan to hang a magnificent portrait of the late President Juarez in the entryway of the Presidential Palace for all of the people to admire. When they see it, they will reflect on just how much he meant to Mexico. Benito was a great friend. When we studied law, he was our tutor, you know. We thought of him as a father, for as it is known, we lost our own when we were but three years of age," he said. His new affectation was using the first person plural "We" for "I" ala European royalty with which his ego equated himself.

The only part of that speech that was true was his father did, in fact, die when he was three leaving his mother poor and alone to raise him and his seven brothers and sisters. As for the rest, everyone had heard the stories that as Benito Juarez became president, Diaz sought to unseat him. His massive ego was damaged when he was not offered an important position in Juarez's new government so he began to plot to take power himself.

Busterman was honored but not awed. He had painted portraits of kings, princes, and presidents for years. Diaz was imposing but not overwhelming, so he graciously accepted the commission. A presidential commission was never a bad thing on one's resume. He promised to deliver it as soon as possible which he reckoned would be within a couple of weeks or so. As he turned to be shown out, the president added, "Senor Busterman, just don't show him sitting on a horse. Everyone is painted on a horse. We ourselves will probably be presented in such a manner. But in dear Benito's case he should be shown at his desk doing what he did best—thinking. He was the greatest thinker among us. We know you will make us proud, adios senor."

Molina returned from escorting the artist through the upper rooms to the staircase. He closed the doors and smiled in his sickeningly sycophantic manner, "That was a wonderful speech my president. I, myself almost believed you loved the conniving Indian hypocrite. I especially liked the part of him sitting at his desk 'thinking' when what you meant was 'plotting.'"

The president rang a small bell for the valet to bring coffee and said thoughtfully, "I did love him…in my own way. He inspired in me my commitment to social justice. If not for him, I would not have been exposed to the Ideals of Liberalism. I would have still been in that seminary learning to be one of God's henchmen. For that, at least, I owe him much. Oh, I've heard the rumors that I was behind the effort to oust him, but that was only small minds conjuring up lies about how they think I probably felt after being betrayed by someone I had fought for. I was a little upset when I was not included in his new government to be sure, but I would never go so far to overthrow an elected president (ignoring the obvious fact that that is precisely what he had just done). Dictators are made from such men, and I embrace the constitution with all my being."

"But he stole the election from you, Excellency!" Molina countered.

"Nonsense, he did nothing the rest of us were not doing. He just had more effective partisans than we did. We learned well and we know now how to never lose another election in the future." His words were prophetic as everyone would discover.

Chapter Nine

Jack was hidden in some rocks watching the three men who approached from a great distance. He slowly raised the Sharps to his shoulder and started to focus the sights when the unmistakable feel of a gun barrel nudged him behind the ear and a familiar female voice say, "Surprise!"

He rolled over and seeing his assailant, he bellowed, "Goddamn it Carolina, what the hell are you doin'?" She was standing there dusty and disheveled with a Winchester and a sly grin on her dirty face.

"What the happy hell are you doin' lass? Why are you sneakin' up on me like this?" he bellowed!

"To show you I can. I wanted to prove to you that all of the lessons you taught me years ago took hold. I'm a pretty good tracker in my own right; good enough to sneak up on you without detection!"

He snarled, "Are you tryin' to get yourself shot to hell."

"Shot—by you? You wouldn't have known I was even behind you if I had not said something to alert you. If I had had bad intentions, you'd be dead this very second."

"Carolina Jacqueline Salcido, you are a precious little girl with evidently some talent, but this ain't women's work. Killin' a man's different than killin' an empty bottle. These targets tend to shoot back which confounds things, I'm tellin'."

"John Jack Rose," she countered, "You haven't been around in years. Do you honestly think I would not have tried to improve after you left? Do you not remember how I loved shooting and would aggravate you to death for the next lesson? You trained me and like you always say, 'just hide and watch' and see what I can do!"

After a moment, a look of sadness crawled across her face and she began to sob. She was trying a new tack in her plan to soften his stance. The effort she had made that day when she first brought it up had failed, but this time it seemed to have worked. He walked up and put his arms around her and held her while she cried. As he held her close, he thought to himself, "My sweet insane Carolina, you have become quite the woman." After a few minutes, he leaned away a little and used the back of his finger to trace the track the tears had made in the dust on her cheeks. He smiled and said softly, "You know you're makin' mud pies on those adorable cheeks, don't you?"

She pulled away from him and was for the first time aware of her appearance. Her beautiful curly reddish-brown hair was scattered all over the place like the haphazard nest of some bizarre bird and she was covered with more dust than she could have gotten if she had been dragged behind her horse. She walked several yards away to where the beast was tied up and retrieved a change of clothes plus some soap and a washcloth. She marched to the river's edge, stripped and plunged under the water.

As she stood in knee deep water soaping herself he tried mightily to be a gentleman and not look but he failed utterly. He felt that he would have to have been the most pious of saints or dead eight days to not be compelled to stare at the magnificent body on the most beautiful woman alive. He sure as hell was no saint and from the stirrings raging around his body, he definitely was not yet dead either. He quite openly drank in the beauty that was Carolina Salcido. He was grinning like a possum passing a peach seed when she turned and saw him downright ogling her.

She stepped onto the shore but made no effort to cover herself. She jammed her fists into her hips and snapped, "Like what you see old man?" She obviously was enjoying that her plan was working. The look on his face told her that she had his complete attention.

He laughed out loud and said, "If I wasn't knowin' anythin' else, I would know you are Margarita's sister by the way you're standin'. She took that pose with me a hundred times. She would never cuss, but her eyes called me a 'dumb-assed bavoso!'"

"I don't believe it!"

"What don't you believe?"

"That she needed to call you a 'dumb-assed bavoso' only one hundred times!" she snickered.

"Now about that 'old man' nonsense," he growled taking a step towards her.

She reached down to her pile of clothes, pulled her pistol and fired a shot between his feet and snapped, "The next one takes your manhood pendeho!"

He jumped back and shouted, "Goddamn it Caro! When I taught you to shoot, it was for your protection against shit like snakes and such!"

"I was shooting at a snake, gringo!" she returned. She holstered her pistol and defiantly dressed at a leisurely pace in order to keep her nude body visible as long as possible. In a highly provocative manner, she adjusted her breasts for several seconds after donning her blouse smiling all the while.

It dawned on him that what she was doing was meant to tease him to the breaking point. Getting control of his rising lust, he shook his head and said, "You know of course, I'm goin' to have to kill you. I can't have no man alive shootin' at me and live to tell about it!"

"Well in case you don't remember what you were drooling over just now, I'm no man!"

"Yeah, and that does seem to confound it a bit" he chuckled. "But let me tell you this little girl, when you prance around in your 'altogethers' in front of a man who has been on the trail a long time, he just may act like a man, I'm tellin'!" he added with a wink.

Over her objections, he told her that he was taking her home for a family meeting. He said there was no way he was going to allow her to tag along without her father's approval, especially after what he had just witnessed. He couldn't guarantee his restraint would prevail again. She acted innocent of his inferences of her intentions. She had merely freshened up in the general area of someone who was something like a brother. It was nothing more devious than that she protested.

As they rode, something came to him and he asked, "You said that even as a child, you knew were goin' to marry me. Well Missy, what the hell did you plan to do with your sister? I seem to remember her bein' in the thick of things."

She smiled and said, "Nothing."

"What the hell does that mean? I ain't the 'two at a time' kind. I ain't real sure I can handle one, I'm thinkin'."

"I mean I wouldn't have to do anything. Margarita was actually afraid of you and would have eventually broken it off. Then you would have seen that I was woman enough for you and let you figure out the rest for yourself."

"Damn lass, you got more twists than a sidewinder in a grass fire! I ain't afraid of anything walkin' upright, but you're startin' to scare the hell out of me, by God!" She hoped so.

That night as they camped well off the trail, four bandits emerged from the dark while they spread their bedrolls. Jack quickly drew his gun as did she which convinced them they had chosen victims unwisely. They beat a hasty retreat back into the darkness.

She turned to him as said, "That was fun!"

He frowned and said, "Fun you say? Lass, four bandits investigatin' our camp ain't what I call fun. It ain't fun havin' to shoot some lowlifes just to get some sleep!"

"Well, it was fun for me. I have never done anything like that. All we had to do was just draw. We didn't have to shoot or anything."

"Four men would have not fled from just one, so I guess when they saw you holdin' your gun that made the difference and they got scared," he teased. "I guess I have to say that you saved me lass, so I'm thankin' you."

She frowned and said, "You don't have to be sarcastic! You do this every day and I don't. It's new for me, so be quiet and let me have my time!"

"I wasn't spoofin'. I mean it; you saved me from a shootout. Anytime bullets are flyin' about, anything can happen. You're never guaranteed that you are goin' to be the one that wins. So thank you goddamn it!"

"Thank you, Jack. That was nice of you to say," she wasn't sure she believed him, but in case he was serious, it was nice to hear.

Jack remained wary for the rest of the night. Aside from worry that the intruders may return, his mind would not leave Carolina. He was conflicted that maybe her machinations meant she actually wanted him after all and he had misunderstood and had given up too easily. He wondered if she would accept his advances if he made them now? But he would be humiliated if he had misinterpreted her actions and she rebuked him for trying to take advantage of the situation. At long last, his mental molestation gave him a headache so he tried to ban such thoughts in order to have a little peace.

She didn't sleep much either but from excitement rather than alertness. Being around him was proving to be everything she had hoped for. Even as an adolescent, she knew that this was what she wanted to do. She wanted to be on the trail with desperate men all about. She had always imagined the excitement of a shootout. Even though the encounter with the four men did not result in gunplay, she had been prepared. She was proud of that. She now had a greater appreciation for what he faced daily. He could not afford to relax his guard for even a second, or it may be his last. She was amazed that a man could live like this. She was amazed a man would have to. She had always admired his manliness and felt safe when he was around, but now she really felt safe and knew he would protect her from all dangers. That was a good feeling in deed. She knew at that moment that she was not finished with this life. She was exhilarated that she had been on the verge of a fight and had not been afraid. She didn't care what her father may say she was going to figure out a way to keep riding with Jack whether either of them liked it or not.

She thought briefly of the bathing incident and realized she had taken it too far. She had merely wished to interest him, and tease him a little but she now thought what she had done was torture for the poor man instead. She admitted to herself that it would have served her right if he had of taken her on the spot, but she was thankful that he was a gentleman and restrained himself. She vowed that she would not be so provocative in the future. She would be coy and flirtatious, but not overly so.

They made their way back to the ranch. The family was greatly relieved that the ordeal was over and Carolina was unharmed. They had tried unsuccessfully to talk her out of following Jack.

The next morning, Jack found Tony alone at breakfast. His custom was to eat early before the family came down so he could read his bi-weekly newspaper in peace. He had a wide grin on his face which prompted Jack to inquire, "Hola, mi patron, and why the smile?"

"Everyone should smile this day! It is in the newspapers; General Porfirio Diaz begins as president. It is a great day for

Mexico! He is a great friend of mine. As young men, we were at the seminary together but he wanted to be a lawyer and I wanted to raise horses, but mostly we wanted to raise the devil."

"Of course I've heard of Diaz, but I don't know much about him. I know less about politics than a possum knows about poker."

"General Diaz is a great war hero! He stopped the French invaders from taking Mexico City. He was wounded and captured but he escaped and fought on and won the day!"

"But I thought them French som-bitches captured Mexico City. I seem to remember that before he managed to get himself shot, that bastard Maximilian runnin' around acting all important and such."

"That is true, but not on that day they didn't. That was May 5th 1862, a great day for us Mexicans. Just the same, General Diaz recaptured it five years later. But let me say, I'm impressed my learned friend."

Jack grinned and said, "I'm afraid you just got the sum total of my Mexican history, I'm thinkin'. Tony, let me ask you this, why is it so important for Diaz to be president?"

"That is easy. First of all, I'm a conservative and a patriot and do not like the way liberals like Benito Juarez sought to gut the power of the army. There was a time when the military had their own court system and handled their affairs internally. But Juarez deemed they were merely trying to circumvent the authority of the civil courts. That is not true, because there are situations where civil authorities should have no jurisdiction, such as 'cowardice in the face of the enemy' or simple disobedience for instance. These are things civilians have no concept of."

"I don't know, but that Juarez bird sounds kinda like an idiot to me, fiddlin' with the army and all. Doesn't he know those lads have the means to sort him out if they've a mind?"

"He's dead now, but Jackie my son," Tony said, "You don't know the half of it. Juarez, as minister of justice, and later Finance minister Miguel Lerdo de Tejada declared it law that the church could no longer hold land. Church real estate would have to be broken up and sold off into private hands as part of the liberal's attempt to diminish the overall power of the church. The state intended to tax such sales for national revenue. Monasteries were closed and nunneries were barred from seeking novices. This, plus wild promises of reform had peasants taking over estates. Men of the church fought to protect their privileged position and isolated Indian villagers, having no politics other than their own community interests, considered everyone other than themselves to be foreigners. They sought to defend their collective lands against government imposed policies. Diaz sees the creation of a modern society unobstructed by communally held property. He feels that the modernization of Mexico could only be achieved through the discipline of authoritarian rule. Diaz plans to restore a centralized government in the capital instead of petty local loyalties. Now all we have is state governors and caudillos keeping control of their little corners of the world by stirring up the masses with promises of social reform."

"Tony, you must think I'm dumber than Tuesday, but I ain't keepin' up real well. What did you say Diaz was doin' about all this silliness?"

"What this means is, by centralizing power back in the capital, we have one Mexico and not dozens of small, private areas of government. You might consider each of these as a country unto itself."

Jack grinned and shook his head and said, "Damn lad, if I tried to keep all that in my head, my brain would look like you had run it through a butter churn. All I know is Diaz dodged bullets, so that's good enough for me. Any man who gets shot at and shoots back for his principals is worthy, by God!" For that reason alone, Jack became something of a sympathetic partisan himself.

Tony took Jack on a ride around his five thousand acre horse ranch. The old man was obviously proud of his hacienda and enjoyed taking guests around whenever the opportunity arose.

Jack had always loved the place and now as they rode, he could see himself retiring and living the good life on a ranch just like this. When he realized what he was thinking, he shook his head in an effort to clear his mind. Men like him have a hard time retiring. There are always young punks, braver than smart, calling them out. But still, it was a nice dream for a minute. Maybe someday he'll actually try to settle down with a nice girl like...Carolina. There, he had admitted it to himself. Since the bathing incident that day, his mind had been completely jumbled. Her body never left his thoughts, and now the idea of possessing that body permanently had bullied its way into his conscious mind and taken root.

He had always thought of her as a sweet girl with a sense of humor, loving and trusting, but a little on the bold side. She had always made him eat his words when he would say, "Girls don't do this or that," but damned if she hadn't grown into a stunningly beautiful woman! The bad news was she was now armed and a good shot to boot! He only had himself to blame for that since he was the one who had taught her to shoot in the first place. This new found wildness and willingness to hunt down bad men intrigued him. It actually added to her attractiveness, but not enough to want to take responsibility for her safety on the trail. But then again, she had called him, "her man" almost constantly but she may have been kidding, knowing the way her mind worked. It was an interesting dilemma to say the least.

Tony interrupted his musings when he said, "Jackie, I must thank you again for protecting my little girl and bringing her home. She is so headstrong and would not listen to her old father. I feared losing a second daughter, but still she insisted. I knew you would not let anything happen to her, but I also realize that it is not your responsibility and at last, I must be a father and demand she give up this wanting to wear a gun. So you must help me in this and when she demands to go with you again, you must refuse. I know she will make it difficult on you but you must stand firm. It would kill me to see her get hurt, or worse." The old man had tears in his eyes as he finished.

Jack's heart went out to him. He knew the old man was at his wit's end and reaching out to him man to man for help. He placed his hand on Tony's arm and said, "She's smart, and I'll bet a two-tailed cat she's up to somethin', but she's a good girl and will come to see that this idea of hers ain't fittin' for a woman. She's headstrong for sure, but I don't think she would purposely defy you. She ain't that kind of girl, I'm thinkin'."

They rode a few more minutes in silence when Jack added, "I don't think you have to worry about her because I'll convince her that it ain't no life for a woman. There ain't much privacy for women's doin's. It is hot and dusty and the only bathin' you can do is givin' yourself a half-assed wash in the river. And the bad men are real and there's plenty of them and they ain't spoofin', they'll blow your goddamned head off. It's hard enough for me to stay alive without worryin' about some knot-head who thinks she wants to be a pistol fighter. No sir, I'll just refuse to take her."

Back at the house, she took the news better than both men had expected. She was not happy of course, but she was resigned to their decision. The tears trickling down her cheeks did not have the same effect as before. Jack was resolute in this, even though the tears nearly destroyed his resolve. Proud of himself, he made his goodbyes and rode off. He thought to himself as he left, "Lass, I'm committed to savin' your life whether you agree or not."

For the next several days, he would stop from time to time and watch back down the trail to see if he was being followed. He usually did it anyway, but now he had more of a need. She had already shown him she was able to track him, and he was worried she would do it again. Eventually he decided that she was not coming, so he resumed his patrol.

He ran across the half-eaten remains of a man hidden in some boulders obviously the victim of an attack by a mountain lion. He examined the body and found he had a pistol and rifle both fully loaded but unfired. He thought out loud to himself, "Lad, what the hell were you concentratin' so hard on that you didn't notice a pissed-off puma about to gnaw on your ass?"

The longer he looked at the face of the man, the more he thought it seemed familiar. He examined the gun belt and saw the name; "Tobias Munro" etched into it. He looked at the wanted posters in his saddlebags and found one on him. "You ignorant som-bitch! You laid there all quiet like gettin' ready to ambush somebody and let this happen to you. Who the hell were you that scared of where you wouldn't fire your gun for fear of alertin' him?" Then it dawned on him that he was probably the intended target and if the victim shot at the puma, he would have been alerted. "You poor bastard…I guess that's what they mean when they say, 'pick your poison.' But boyo, a bullet to the forehead is a hell of a lot less painful that what happened to you don't you see?"

He buried the remains and took the gun belt to turn in for the reward, providing the judge accepted it as proof of death. He offered some last words over the grave including some for the puma, "thank you lad, if I could, I'd owe you one…amen."

Chapter Ten

Shafer handed Jack a report of a shooting at a ranch some fifty miles northeast of El Paso, he said, "Some poor cowhand got himself shot returning some strays to where they belonged. It seems the bastard that owned them decided he was stealing them instead so his hired gun shot the poor so and so. I need you to look into it and see just why this son-of-a-bitch thinks he needs a hired gun in the first place. Go be a 'real' lawman and make sure that he isn't putting together an outfit like those border riffraff you're doing something about. And while you're at it, see what the local sheriff is about. Find out why he can investigate a shooting on..." he looked at the report again searching for a name, "oh yes, how can he investigate a shooting of J. O. Robert's man on Robert's own ranch and nothing comes of it. That kind of makes my teach itch. I'm curious as to what that man's understanding of his job is. But I'm sure just you asking him about it will clear it up for him pronto."

"Well hell judge, can I shoot anybody?" he laughed.

"Them that needs it, you know that. But try to hear everybody's side first," he teased. He had no real fears about sending Jack to investigate an actual legal dispute. He knew Jack was smart enough to figure it out, or bring them in if he can't.

Jack gathered Roberts and rode to the giant ranch owned by an Englishman named Thornton Longwood. As they approached the house there were six men standing and sitting around the front porch one of which was obviously Longwood. He was unarmed, well dressed and displayed an air of superiority which deepened when he heard Jack's Irish brogue.

"Since you're the only one I see here smart enough to know to wipe his ass when he's done, you must be Longwood?" rudely stating the obvious.

"Yes, I'm Thornton Longwood, marshal."

"Well Longwood," ignoring politeness "you want to tell me why your punk shot and killed this man's drover returning your cattle? And why does a cattle ranch need a punk in the first place?" he asked glaring at the man with a tied down gun leaning against a post. None of the men looked like drovers and were probably professionals, but the one he addressed looked like the one they took their lead from.

"Marshal," he said disgustedly like the word stuck in his mouth, "this man was stealing my cattle. He is lucky he was not shot himself. He claims his man was returning my herd, but it didn't look like it from where I was sitting. We've had trouble with him and his men in the past which is why I have been forced to hire some specialists."

Jack turned to Roberts and asked, "Is that true lad, were you stealin' his cattle?" The man explained that strays often mix in with his herd and when he finds them, he always chases them back. Jack looked at Longwood and continued, "He says you're lyin'. Cows are naturally stupid and can't read a map real good but if they're pointed in the direction of your ranch, I'd bet a two-tailed cat they were goin' home. So since you say it didn't like it from where you were sittin', just where the happy hell were you sittin'? Sounds like you were trespassin' to me, but I ain't here to be figurin' the rightness of it, my job is to make sure everybody learns to be good citizens, and warn them that needs it."

The gunman stood up straight and said coldly, "Warn about what?"

Jack grinned as if he had waited to the gunman to join in the conversation, "Warn folks that the judge is a hard man and fair, but he does like to hang folks, especially 'specialists', if they live long enough to stand in front of him, that is. Does that answer your question?"

"Not really. I'm just curious if one of us decides we're not going with you to see the judge, what are you going to do about that?"

"Lad, I'll be a two-headed yellow spider if I thought you were really wantin' an answer to that stupid question!"

"I've never heard of a marshal issuing threats to honest citizens protecting their property." Longwood interjected.

Jack glared at the Englishman and said, "Well your worship, there you go. You see I ain't what you'd call a regular deputy US marshal. I'm what the judge called a 'gatekeeper'. I decide who sees the judge and if they get to El Paso on his horse or tied across it."

The gunman took a step forward and said, "Are you threatening Mr. Longwood?"

Jack dismounted but the Englishman defused the growing tension with a dismissive wave of his hand to his man.

"You see Roberts, these are nearly intelligent men but I'm sure they all got the message the judge wanted them to get. The next time you have to shoo Longwood's ignorant cattle back where they belong, these lads will just smile and say 'thank you'. Won't you lads?"

Longwood said he could have Jack's job for threatening him, to which Jack replied he had never seen a real threat if he thought that was one. He added, "The judge ain't goin' to be firin' me your worship on account of he likes the way I settle disputes, all neat and tidy like. There's usually ain't nothin' for him to do but make funeral arrangements, but I'm thinkin' you can try him if you've a mind." He then looked directly into the gunman's eyes and snarled, "Lad, the judge did say I could kill them that needed killin'." With that he pulled his gun so fast the man had no time to react but he didn't fire, instead he said, "You see punk, even on your best day you ain't ready for me. A wise lad would be grateful for the warnin' and behave himself. Of course you don't look particularly wise, so what say we do it again?" He holstered his pistol and stood grinning in front of the startled gunman. The man slowly smiled and folded his arms across his chest and made no effort to inflame the situation further.

Satisfied that peace was made all round, he mounted and left Longwood's property. He advised Roberts to make sure his men were careful especially concerning the boundary between ranches. He said he didn't favor a range war, but he urged Roberts to not let men ride that area alone. He said he was going to stop by the local sheriff's office and help clear up any questions that mongrel may have about doing his job. Since he did nothing about the first episode, he was probably in league with Longwood, but he would know for sure by the time he left.

Roberts was still in awe and said, "That was stunning. I'm amazed that you refrained from pulling the trigger since it was obvious you were angry enough. I have never seen anything as fast in my life. You were a blur."

"Liked it did you lad? I knew that I didn't have to fire since it was obvious that showin' him the difference between the men and the boys would do nice like. Lad, in any group of men, most are just there to watch but there's always one who is committed to pushin' things. That's the man you have to convince of his folly. By the way, reckon he pissed himself?" he laughed.

Chapter Eleven

President Diaz was preparing to step out at the rear of his railcar to make a speech to the people of Juarez. In celebration of the end of his second year in office, he was making a journey by train to visit as much of the country as possible. As he stood admiring his reflection in the full-length mirror a disturbance sprang up on the loading platform outside. The commotion broke through the door at the head of the car and into the presence of the president. Several members of his army's security unit were trying to subdue the powerfully built angry redheaded man they were endeavoring to escort inside.

The startled president asked, "Huerta, what is the meaning of this?"

"Excellency, this man was lurking in the crowd. He is the famous shootist, Jack Rose of Texas," the commander of the unit replied.

"No sir, I wasn't lurkin' goddamn it, I came with the Garcia family to see you! They knew it wouldn't be that often they'd get a chance to see the president himself. And I admit I was a bit curious myself."

He waved his hand to his men to release Jack and said, "You must forgive Captain Huerta, he is in charge of our security unit and as you see, he is very good at what he does. And give him back his gun belt because from what I have heard of this man, if he had wanted us dead, you would already be attending to our body." He extended his right hand and motioned for Jack to have a seat with his left.

Jack returned the handshake and said sheepishly, "And you must forgive me, your honor, I've not talked to a government man except a judge, a time or two so I may not get things just right." He laid his gun belt across his lap as he sat down.

Captain Huerta added, "This man was once to be married to the daughter of Antonio Gomez de la Salcido. She was murdered recently and her suspected killers were more or less executed without trial."

"Lad, you're startin' to rile me! They received God's own justice! Hell, your goddamned police couldn't do it, it's a wonder those gutless idiots didn't join sides with that murderin' scum! There's more bandits around here than flies—what are you doin' about that boyo?"

The president calmed the growing tension with a grin and said, "Captain, any man who is good enough for the daughter of Tony Salcido, is good enough for us. You see what we mean when we say Captain Huerta is very good at what he does? He keeps more information in his head than we have in the books in our library. Thank you captain, that will be all," he said dismissing Huerta. "Tony and I were friends many years ago. We were young and ignorant, but he has done well."

"It would seem that you have too, your honor. I bet bein' president ain't a bad job itself."

"You say your friends are among the crowd? Please ask them to come in Senor Rose. I always enjoy meeting voters, especially if they voted for me" he laughed.

Jack stepped out on the rear platform and motioned for the Garcia's to join him. After introductions, the president noticed the look of puzzlement on the face of Reyes and said, "Please Senor Garcia, do not be concerned for your friend. The captain of our security unit sometimes gets ahead of himself. We were merely welcoming Senor Rose to Mexico. We always have a place for a man of his...his skills. Who knows what the future will bring. Maybe we will have need of those skills one day. Now you must excuse us, there are people who want to hear a speech and since we are already here…" he let his words tail off and shrugged his shoulders as if put upon.

Jack stood and said, "Just let me know if you ever need my help your hon…er…Excellency," he had finally figured out the proper form of address.

As they reached the door, the president added, "Senor Rose, please feel free to visit us at the palace whenever you are in the capital and Senor Garcia, thank you for your vote, but if you didn't, I know you will next time."

"Yes Excellency" Reyes lied. He was the kind of poor farmer that Diaz's programs specifically sought to eliminate. He had merely come to see the man in the flesh and hear the speech with his own ears and not second hand from some agitator. They returned to the crowd and listened to the thirty minute address then rode home afterwards.

As the train pulled away from the station, Huerta entered the car and sat opposite from the president. "Excellency, that man Jack Rose is dangerous and has killed many men. I must caution; you should be extremely careful around him."

"Nonsense! We have heard the same stories as you. He was nothing more than a policeman, a crude and violent one to be sure, but a policeman just the same."

"But Excellency, they say he has killed over forty men, some of which from a great distance with a high powered rifle. What kind of policeman does that?"

"A prudent one. From what we know of this, he was charged with stopping dangerous men from entering Texas and sometimes the means can by necessity, be rather harsh. Maybe someday we will have need of his services keeping these undesirables out of Mexico instead. Our plan is to make Mexico so attractive that we may need border guards to stop the flow the other way. Of course what he said about the scourge of banditry is true; maybe we can use him there in some capacity."

"But Excellency, for appearances sake you should not be seen as being too friendly with men of his ilk."

"Huerta, Huerta, we have not made any decisions yet, we are merely thinking ahead. Just the reputation alone of such a man could be of value if used wisely. But like we said, we are merely thinking out loud." He dismissed Huerta wanting to enjoy the trip to the next stop and the next speech.

Huerta stood between cars for several minutes. He decided the president had it right and he too should find a way to use this man for his own purposes. Jack went on his list of men to watch at that very moment. He muttered to himself as he entered the next car, "We'll just see about you, Senor Gringo Gunman."

Chapter Twelve

On a frequent visit a few months later, Jack sat with Reyes in the shade under a large tree just out the front door of the house. The simple dwelling was surrounded on three sides by corn and beans. Reyes said he raised sufficient amounts for the family and just enough extra to sell in Juarez for the few pesos the family realized. If he had much more of a crop, the bandits would find it attractive to rob him thinking he had more money than he did. He explained that ironically in keeping his farm small to protect himself, it is in danger of being confiscated and resold to foreign investors in an effort to create giant modern corporate farms. He showed Jack an order to come before a government magistrate in a week's time where he would find out the decision.

Jack was beside himself and said, "That's the sorriest, damnedest thing I ever heard! You mean them som-bitches can throw you off your property and give it to some other som-bitch, without a 'by your leave'?"

"Yes, most of the small farms here have been confiscated already. The rest are like mine; soon to be taken. The president has proclaimed many times that economic progress is the most important issue he faces. I am worried, for my family has nowhere else to go. My family has lived on this land for generations and now we are in danger of being homeless."

Jack jumped up and snapped, "You ain't goin' nowhere just yet. I'm goin' to Juarez and catch the night train to Mexico City and see if I can talk to the president about this. He acted like he wanted us to be amigos, well here's his chance."

Anna had been sitting quietly with them and she too stood and approached Jack and appeared to want to kiss his cheek but planted one on his lips instead. He blushed instantly and babbled, "Lass! What are you doin'? I ain't complainin' you understand, that was awful nice, but your daddy is watchin'. You want to get me shot?" It was not their first kiss, but it was the first in front of her father.

"That is for what you are doing for us. We are grateful, more than we can say. And don't worry about my father; he knows how I feel about you. I have told him often enough. When you get back, I'll tell you" she smiled.

*   *   *   *

The president fumed as he sat at his massive mahogany desk reading the report that the French ambassador had said that the only Mexican institution that functioned with "perfect regularity" was banditry. It was an old saw, but it was making the rounds again in subversive newspapers and the penny press. The president was afraid such comments along with raids into northern Mexico from the apaches of Geronimo and Victorio would hinder foreign investment. But as luck would have it, the greatest calming influence he could think of just showed up without a summons. He felt it was fortuitous to say the least.

Jack was shown into the president's office and given a seat. Diaz walked over to the bar setup in the corner and asked, "What do you drink?"

Jack smiled and said, "Tequila Excellency, but not until after we talk. When I get to suckin' on that pleasantness, I've been known to agree to some pretty strange things, I'm thinkin'. But first, beggin' your pardon, I have a problem you might can help me with. Do you remember the Garcia family you met that day on the train in Juarez?" The president nodded in the affirmative, then he continued, "They've got a notice from some magistrate or another in Juarez to defend their right to the pitiful patch of dirt they call home. They've lived there since there was a Mexico. Can you do something for them? I'd owe you one if you could." Diaz smiled and said, "Done." He pulled a document from his desk and wrote a few quick words, affixed his seal, signed it and handed it to Jack. It was a presidential proclamation absolving the Garcia's from any and all actions current or future and deeded them the property in perpetuity. "Damn Excellency, that's great of you. I was hopin' you could help a little, like makin' that mongrel in Juarez back off a tad, but this is more than I had imagined. Thank you very much. Now what can I do to return the favor? Want me to shoot Huerta?" he teased.

Diaz grinned and began, "Oddly enough, there is a favor that I need, and no, it is not shooting Captain Huerta...just yet anyway, but I do have need of a service that is not so difficult for you, since you are known for it already."

"It'll be an honor Excellency, but I don't know what services I could provide you with that you don't already have in aces's all."

"Well what I don't have 'in aces,' as you say, is an experienced man to stand against the growing scourge of banditry in the state of Chihuahua, where these very Garcia's in fact live, if I'm not mistaken. We have decided on a plan to eradicate these vermin. If we are ever going to secure investment to expand our economy, people must trust that their investment is safe. People are reluctant to put up money when bandits and apaches are running amok making life difficult. We want you to lead this operation, if you please." As he spoke, he began writing something on another piece of paper.

"Hell lad," he started then realizing it was inappropriate, "sorry...but you've got an army large enough to invade Texas if you've a mind, so why don't you just turn them loose on these som-bitches? I'd have them fan out shoulder to shoulder and stroll from one ocean to the other shootin' anyone who didn't look just right."

"But Jack, having the appearance of a military state is the only thing that would inspire less confidence among investors. The army is always a threat to revolt and can't be trusted anyway. As far as the Indians are concerned, the army will be sufficient in size to harass them back across the border, and provide peace of mind for the population but not look like an invasion. But for the bandits of your precious Chihuahua, we propose an elite force of ten men from the rurales led by you to take care of the problem in whatever fashion you choose."

"You may think I'm stupid or something, but again, you've got men for that, so why me? I'm not tryin' to get out of my debt to you, but I'm just askin'."

"Let me ask you this, if you were a bandit which words would you be more afraid of hearing; 'Captain Lopez or Captain Garcia is looking for you', or 'Fast Jack Rose is hunting you?' We know who would get our attention and no disrespect to Captains Lopez and Garcia, but your name strikes fear in the heart's of men. And this is the message we wish to send. If you are a bandit in northern Mexico, you are at risk."

Jack leaned back in his chair and asked, "Tell me about this elite force."

"They are, for the most part, former bandits and gunmen themselves so they are familiar with the life and habits of the men they chase."

"Former bandits? I'll be a two-tailed cat if I think that's a good idea. When the shootin' starts, they may decide to take sides with their old pals and shoot at me instead!"

"My dear Jack that will not happen we assure you. These men were selected for their skills which are similar to your own. They shoot quite well and are fearless in the face of danger. They are loyal and they know they will be shot for treason if they do not perform their duties to the utmost. If that is not motivation enough, they know we will destroy their families in retaliation.

That may sound barbaric to you, but sometimes inducing loyalty from savages, calls for savagery itself. This is war and we are committed to winning. Will you consider assisting us in this endeavor?" He then handed the second paper to Jack and smiled as he waited for him to read what he had written. It was a document awarding Jack Mexican citizenship.

Jack sat speechless for several seconds before he said, "You know of course, I am honored, but if you don't mind, I'll be havin' that drink now. If I have to get on that train and go to El Paso and be tellin' that infernal Judge Shafer that I'm no longer a deputy US marshal because President Diaz himself made me a Mexican policeman, I'll be needin' more than one drink, I'm thinkin'. I'll bet a two-headed cat that'll be an interestin' conversation."

Diaz laughed and said, "Done and done," he then told him that his detachment is already at the station waiting to board the train. Jack grinned because the president was like the judge thinking he was predictable and easy to manipulate, which he admittedly was. He had made another dramatic change in his life on the spur of the moment with absolutely no hesitation or thinking it through. He wondered why he was not afraid of any man alive, yet he could not say no to powerful men. He decided to wait until the next time he got drunk to ponder that particular character flaw. They shook hands and Jack left.

Diaz then bellowed for Molina to gather the ever present ministers from the outer office and a stenographer and attend him immediately. Soon the room teemed with finely tailored uniforms replete with copious amounts of ornate gold braiding and large hats with exaggerated feathery plumes.

The agenda was a report sent by undercover agents of the army of the growing unrest in the state of Chihuahua. The report told of meetings that had begun with three disgruntled artisans and over the past few weeks have grown to nearly fifty. They had been unable to compete with new government run factories for the sale of their handmade goods in a free market environment. Farm laborers have been forced off the countryside and into manufacturing driving the local artisans to either join them or perish.

The president looked onto a room full of faces puzzled as to why they had been summoned, but glad of the opportunity to strut in front of others of their station. "I have received a report of meetings in Chihuahua that are a cause of great concern for all in this room."

"What kind of meetings, Excellency?" asked the army's Chief of Staff, General Sandoval, who made a mental note to find out why his staff had not seen fit to show him the report before passing it on.

"The secret kind of meeting that seems to spring from the soil in Chihuahua like any other crop. Three men, a Pedro Rodriguez, a Julio Salya, and a Nicholas Sandoval," he said peering down at his notes. He looked up and asked, "Any relation general?"

"No Excellency, my family is from Guadalajara, as your Excellency is aware. But it is a common enough name." he quickly blurted out.

The president grinned and said, "Have you grown so comfortable in your position that you now tell us of what we are aware?" He paused a second or two for effect and continued, "Relax general. We served with your father and brothers at Puebla and know very well where you are from. We just couldn't help trying to get a rise out of you. The men of your family are very brave and loyal, as are you, but the three men on this list are not so loyal. They secretly gather other men and criticize our policies and programs for the welfare of our people. According to this message, they take issue with our handling of our indigenous population. They insist that these people should keep their land to use as they see fit and not be forced off making way for trained agronomists building profitable corporate farms." He slammed his open hand on his desk startling those in attendance. Few, if any, had ever seen him in such a state of anger. "These...these people grow nothing, they produce nothing, the only use they have for the land is a place for their goats to graze! They cannot grow enough to feed themselves let alone growing enough to feed others. Their land barely supports the goats! These people do not know modern techniques of farming. They have never heard of modern techniques, they do not even want to know. The lands are being turned into large modern farms and will eventually feed the nation with plenty to spare. Dams are being built and irrigation systems are underway. Soon Mexico will be green and not brown."

He sat back down and returned his attention to the issue at hand. "Now we must see to these malcontents in Chihuahua. It seems that in that accursed state, political negativism is passed down through their mother's milk," he smiled at the laughter about the room. "These...these...men seek to gather disgruntled men by incessant negativism. Let us impress the people with the power of Positivism. Positivism is nothing new and has been around for decades, but we are dusting off the word and going to wield it as a club. It is obvious we prize economic development regardless the cost...especially the cost of credibility to these gainsayers. It is our thinking that it must be shown that only when economic stability is achieved, can progress begin on social conditions and not the reverse as preached by the socialist trade unionists. When men are well fed, they are not so inclined to listen to agitators, especially from the trouble makers from these radical unions. It is hard to convince a man with a full belly that he doesn't have it so good. To ensure that the economy grows and is healthy, we must protect and encourage the flourishing of the haciendada. They are the real economic backbone of the nation. They provide for the critical needs of the people by the raising of cattle, horses and sheep and other needed products. They provide jobs for many thousands. Therefore to encourage even greater growth, diligence and loyalty of this class of men, we hereby absolve them of any further tax burden levied on their operations. They are free to reinvest their profits back into their haciendas for the improvement of goods and services as they see fit. They know better than anyone what their needs may be. So let them grow their businesses and drag these burros along with them into economic prosperity, whether or not they wish to go. The mills, mines and factories will flourish when staffed with competent workers and we are integrated into the world economy."

He nodded acknowledgement to the applause from the assembled ministers, many of whom came from just that class. He glanced back down to his list and began, "And now for benefit of Senores Rodriguez, Salya and Sandoval, we declare that political discussions in groups of more than two people are hereby forbidden," he looked up and laughed, "We only wish we could figure out a way to stifle those who talk sedition only to themselves! We had an aunt who talked to herself, but she was a loyalist and not a threat, at least we haven't had to shoot her just yet." After the laughter subsided he continued, "The punishment for the violation of this decree is imprisonment, or worse!" He winked at the stenographer and said not to include that last part then resumed, "We wonder what that will do for attendance at their little get-togethers?"

He noticed a smallish slight-built man in a colonel's uniform with his hand raised, "Yes colonel?"

The man's high-pitched voice was barely audible when he spoke, "Excellency, our constitution guarantees the freedom of speech. How do you plan to resolve the legality of your decree?"

"Who are you? We've not seen you before."

"I am Colonel Samuel de Alonzo. I am legal advisor to General Sandoval's staff. My area is Constitutional Law, Excellency."

"My dear Colonel de Alonzo, the constitution is the most important document man can possess. It is what makes us civilized men and not barbarians. We ourselves have fought and bled for ours. Men live by their wits but nations live by laws. A nation cannot exist except for laws, no matter how crafty the men of that nation may be. For the time being, Mexico needs order above all else. This country is consumed with local loyalties based on group identities and not a universal image shared by all. All citizens should receive the same training so their ideals can be merged into a national identity. Then and only then can the type of economic development be addressed which will bring along all men, regardless of their politics. When our economy is thriving and we are standing on our two feet, you will see today's decree will be allowed to expire quietly. But for now, we cannot afford to have negativists gainsay our economic strivings. Political free-speech in backrooms is less important than food on the table. No one believes in the constitution more deeply than us, but we are willing to sacrifice our ideals temporarily for the good of the many. We appreciate your concerns, but you will see we are correct in this, so thank you and goodbye gentlemen."

Satisfied that by the day's actions, he had addressed his two main promises to the people of wealth and security. He rose from behind his desk and left the room followed closely by his constant shadow, Molina. Later that day when the documents were ready, he signed them into law and retired for the night. As he prepared for bed, his thoughts went to the three conspirators in Chihuahua and he muttered to himself, "Well my friends, you have gotten away with your hate for the last time. You will find that when next you conspire, it will have costs, and those costs will be dear indeed!" With that, he went to bed and slept.

Chapter Thirteen

The judge took the news well and thanked Jack for his years of service and again reminded him to be careful and not be caught up in the political machinations of powerful men. He liked the old man but something tugged at him as he thought the judge was not upset in the least and did not try to talk him out of his new job. He had expected more of an uproar at the news, and was surprised that there was not even a half-hearted attempt to dissuade him. The judge merely smiled and shook hands and patted him on the back as he left the office.

After returning from surrendering his badge in El Paso, Jack led his contingent up to the Garcia home much to the surprise of the family. When they saw the rurales, they were instantly afraid that they were being arrested for something, but when they saw Jack at the head of the formation, they were relieved.

He was dressed the same as the other men in the fanciful charro costumes of the Mexican cowboy. Seeing him in a rurale uniform was cause for no little excitement for Chato and Pedro. He introduced the men as "Rose's Thorns" as one of the men had thought up. He explained his new job to the family and produced his citizenship papers as well. After they were properly impressed, he handed Reyes the presidential proclamation. He thought the man was going to faint! Reyes and his sons grabbed his hands and began kissing them until he said he wasn't the "bloody pope." He told Reyes that before he left the capital, he had the document registered with the courts. Anna just stood there beaming her approval of her man.

He smiled back at Anna. He had thought of almost nothing else but her for the last few days. He was in his mid-thirties and for some time, the thought of settling down and starting a family had been gnawing its way into his consciousness. That day several months ago when he talked of it with Tony was not the first or last time the idea had presented itself. The consequence of this new development was he was confronted with the selection of a possible mate from among three women.

This internal debate began with mountainous anxiety because he had never been faced with selecting from such a menu before. In fact, he had never pondered a decision of any nature more than a few seconds in his life. Now he saw why he never contemplated anything; reflection was an angst filled experience not to mention the attendant labors. His selection process started with Anna. She was beautiful in a sweet, simple way. She was medium in height with black hair and deep dark brown eyes. She was solidly put together, but not muscular. She had marvelous breasts hinting their existence beneath her peasant's blouse. Her sexuality was compelling including her amazingly sexy and husky voice. Just listening to her talk was arousing.

Carolina on the other hand was stunningly beautiful and was taller with stately grace, and she too had nice breasts which he had seen that day at the river. Delia also had a beautiful face and body, but she had a past, and he didn't want to spend his life wondering if each man they passed had ever been with his wife. He instinctually knew that given his volatile temper, the chances of it ending badly were great. He realized that it wasn't fair, especially since he was the one she was now solely involved with, but he reluctantly eliminated her from his equation.

He had also eliminated Carolina, but for different reasons. She was younger, and bent on carving out a wild existence for herself in a man's world. There was nothing wrong with that, but he was beginning to see the need for a more traditional woman in his life. One who loved him and he could count on unconditionally.

Therefore his mental calculations had arrived at Anna as the perfect woman. The deciding factor against the other two women was his reluctance to deal with the constant mental competition with strong-willed women. They demanded their place in a man's world, but Anna demanded nothing. He was pleased with his gyrations and decided he had made the best choice he could ever expect to make. He was well satisfied with his choice and in keeping with his "why wait" personality, thought there was no time like the present to tell her of his intentions.

She went into the house and began to prepare a meal for the men, and Jack followed a few minutes later. She stopped what she was doing and gave him a long hard kiss. As he held her, he said, "You said somethin' about tellin' me how you were feelin'."

She frowned slightly and said, "If you have not figured it out by now, you are not as smart as I thought." She then returned to cooking.

He stood there blushing before he said, "I'll be a two-headed yellow spider if I don't feel the same way, I'm thinkin'. But when did you know?"

She smiled coyly and said, "That first day. When we all sat around talking, I could see that you were a good man, despite your reputation as a ruthless gunman. I could see you becoming important in my life, at least I hoped you would be. A woman wants a man in her life that she knows will protect her and provide for her children if she should have any. And when did you start to have feelings for me?"

Jack grinned widely and said, "During the same conversation lass." He told a little white lie, he didn't know it then, but the process had started at that moment. "I liked the way you wiggled when you walked. Of course, the way you filled out your blouse didn't hurt, I'm tellin'. I like my women full-growed" he teased. He continued, "Seriously, you've not left my mind for a minute since. My mind's been a mess lately, but your face kept showin' up just when I needed it, by god. There comes a time when a man must settle down and get on with the rest of his life. He wants a woman he can trust and lean on when he has a need. The more I thought about you, the more I knew I wanted to spend the rest of my life with the most important woman alive. Besides, I love the hell out you, knot-head!"

They kissed again and he rejoined the men in the front room. That night Jack and the men camped outside beside the house. He told Reyes that they'd be leaving early in the morning on patrol, but when they returned, he would have something to talk to him about of a serious nature.

He put his arm around his smiling daughter's shoulder and beating Jack to the punch said, "Of course you have my permission my friend. She has told me for days that this moment would come soon. I am surprised she did not ask you first, if truth be known."

"Well what do say lass?" He realized that that had not been the most romantic proposal a man has ever offered, but he was in the presence of his men, and was slightly embarrassed for them to see him in such a position.

She smiled and blushed lightly in front of the men and said, "Si mi corazon, of course I will my heart." Then she laughed, "Are all of them moving in with us?"

He grinned, "We'd make a nice little family, I'm thinkin'. Just think, on your weddin' day, you'll be gettin' a husband and ten sons to boot!" Even the men groaned at that one.

In the morning, they rode for the first stop—Delia's.

Chapter Fourteen

"Father, this is Juana. I found her sitting by the stream behind the house. She is from a village near Oaxaca where President Diaz is from," Carolina said as she introduced the two.

Tony studied the Indian woman for several seconds. The poor thing was barefoot and very dirty and the rags passing for a dress she wore had new patches on top of old. She was obviously humbled by her surroundings but gladly drank the glass of water Carolina offered. When finished, she looked at him waiting for him to speak. He could not even formulate a question since he had no idea why she had been brought to him in the first place. He looked to his daughter for a lead.

"Her lands were confiscated and...Juana, you tell it."

"When my husband went to the judge to complain, he was arrested and I could not find where they had taken him. They did not answer my questions and told me I was to be arrested myself if I did not leave there. I then heard that my husband and many other men were shot so I became afraid and ran away and walked here. I finally could walk no more when the senorita found me and brought me here."

"Shot...he was shot for asking a question? I don't believe it! There must be more to the story than that."

"It is true, I swear it."

"I didn't mean I don't believe you, it's just that I don't believe there are secret courts. There must be some other explanation. You say you walked here from Oaxaca, where were you going?" he asked trying to change the subject away from questioning the existence of secret courts, which he knew for a fact did exist.

"I don't know senor. I have no place to go, so I walked." She sadly added, "There seems to be no place for me. Maybe God is angry and won't let me find a place to be. I was born on that land. My father's, father's, father was also born on that land, and now they tell me there is no room for me on that land. How can this be?"

Carolina had been sitting taking it all in even though Juana had already told her the story. With tears in her eyes she said, "Juana, can you wait outside?"

As the woman went out on the veranda, she turned and said, "You know what this means of course."

"What do you think it means?" he snapped. It always aggravated him when she began a conversation with that question. He always inferred from it that she felt she had the only correct point of view which more and more seemed to be the case.

She started patiently, "When the poorest among us cannot seek help from the government, who can they turn to?"

"I am not a child so quit asking questions and tell me what you got on your mind!"

"Don't you see father? A government is there for the protection of the people. It is to provide things that they cannot provide for themselves. Like for instance, an army for protection from foreign enemies and the police and courts. It is to protect the peasants from someone stealing their land. But when the government is the one stealing the land, who can the peasants turn to for protection? I'll tell who, they turn to men who need issues but offer no answers other than the use of arms; and that is where the danger lay. You know all about men with guns and what they are capable of. You have faced groups of four, six, and even ten men. Can you imagine what a group of thousands can do?"

He snarled, "How did you get from some poor Indian woman to a full out revolution without any steps in between?"

"You really don't see it do you? Diaz thinks of himself as the 'patriarch' enforcing his peace demanding political stability which in turn will spur economic development. But father, you cannot simply demand a country be politically stable, you must allow it to become so by letting democracy work. Democracy cannot exist when one man makes all of the laws and decides who is to prosper and what is to become of those chosen to fail. The potential for disaster is great when the government becomes a dictatorship and walks on the backs of the poorest; for that alone, he is morally indefensible. First it was little steps by passing laws that affect these people; then more laws; then even more laws until these people have no political voice and nowhere else to turn. Hopeless people will turn to anyone who they think will help them. Men in the government are getting rich by selling confiscated church land to foreigners and stealing the lands of the peasants to make large private farms that make money for foreigners but do not feed Mexicans!"

Seated in massive high-backed leather chairs facing each other in front of a rock fireplace that took up the entire north wall of great room of the house, Tony listened politely and patiently to his daughter's jejune questioning of political matters she had never before shown any interest in but suddenly, were beginning to poke their way into her consciousness. The largeness of the room with its twenty foot ceilings and huge twelve foot tall oaken double doors always lent the air of authority to any pronouncements this wise, politically astute man made.

"My daughter, it is true the plight of the poor woman is indeed sad, but there are other considerations at hand."

"When men say 'other considerations,' they mean they are trying to make excuses for what they have done. Someone has won and is telling someone else why they had needed to lose based on these mysterious 'other considerations.'"

"It's easy to dismiss another's actions out of hand," Tony continued patiently, "but as a middle class Mexican, you must have an understanding of the issues of class distinction. These people, while tragic, are basically ignorant superstitious savages concerned with only the issues of their own pueblo, and for nearly a century in this country, social liberals have sought to assimilate them into a common culture from the top down. Simply decreeing it into law did not make it so. The president has rightly begun social transformation from the bottom up through public education and not the parochial approach of the Catholic Church. Only then can they be social assets by working in the mills and mines where they are needed. They own small unproductive farms or squat on communal lands that taken together consume vast amounts of land that could be much more productive and feed millions if approached with modern concepts. The president has instituted programs to create large productive farms and sadly, someone had to sacrifice their personal holdings for the better good. The rights of the few cannot outweigh the needs of the many."

"You sound just like him, in fact, the words are his. Did you memorize one of his speeches?"

"Don't be rude! Of course I have read his writings as should you. Diaz is president of all Mexicans; the proletariat, the elite class, and even the peasant and native classes. The president is a great man who has a vision for Mexico to take her place among other great nations. He has instituted programs to build dams for irrigation that will produce enough food to make us not only self-sustaining, but exporters as well. He has promised to build railroads to ship goods and produce to every corner of the country. And he is building telegraphs to connect every village and town with the cities. He has proposed building a system of roads for the convenience of the people."

Carolina interrupted, "You mean for the convenience of the bandits. All that 'new road' nonsense will do is to funnel the pigeons into single file to make it easier for the cats to get at! Banditry is the biggest problem this country faces. Now I'd be impressed if he did something about that."

"My daughter, we as a nation must be patient. The president faces many problems. We cannot expect him to solve them all at once. We must all shoulder the burden. I am sad for this woman, I truly am. As a Christian, I could not be otherwise, but that aside, this is what I mean by 'other considerations'."

As they finished their conversation, Nettie came from the other room leading a shy Juana. She had washed up and put on one of Nettie's old dresses. She said, "Juana is the new housekeeper. We have a need for her services and she has a need for this family."

Tony snorted, "I thought I was the patron around here!"

Nettie, merely replied, "You are out there," she pointed, "but not in here. The hacienda is yours but the house is mine."

Chapter Fifteen

The men all said they liked their new assignment, especially since their first stop was a cantina. They also liked their new commander, Captain Rose, though he didn't like the sound of it and insisted they merely call him Jack. They compromised and called him Captain Jack, which soon became, "El Capitan Fast Jack." He told them they were allowed a few drinks, but not to get drunk. He warned them against saying anything about Anna, or he would shoot them himself. He wanted Delia to hear it from him and not some loose talk at the bar.

He called a laughing Delia aside to tell her of his news. It was only right that he tell her to her face, but he could not make her stop long enough to listen. She was tickled that the great Jack Rose, the ultimate 'loner' was now in the uniform of the rurales.

She giggled, "What's the matter, did the US government go out of business?"

"No goddamn it, I'm doin' this as a favor to Porfirio Diaz himself!"

She laughed even louder, "Well, I didn't know you and the president were such good amigos."

He frowned and snapped, "There's lots of things you don't know about me, I'm thinkin'. Like I'm getting' married in a couple of weeks for one thing!" He instantly regretted being so brutally forthcoming. It was not as he had wished to tell her. He should have used more tact, but there it was.

She leaned back in her chair and said softly, "You son of a bitch! I never asked for much from you because I always knew you held my past against me, but I had imagined you to be more of a gentleman and not just spit in my face like this. Do you respect me so little as that? I knew it wouldn't last forever, but I had expected better from you when it came time to part. And I definitely did not see it ending so rudely. I thought we would just drift apart...but still friends."

Delia was stunned by his clumsy announcement. She had had no clear vision where their relationship would lead. She knew it wouldn't end in marriage, neither seemed to be the type. But somehow, she had seen them sharing their lives in a significant way for some time to come. After they had reached a certain stage and a certain age, they would just drift away with their memories. A former gunfighter and a former whore were a naturally suited pair from the angle of not making judgments about each other's past.

She hadn't always felt so. The first time she saw him, she was repelled by his brash cockiness. She didn't like him and hoped he would not choose her for his night's pleasure. She was disappointed because he did choose her, in fact she was the only he ever picked. He developed a real attachment to her, mainly from familiarity. He was always uncomfortable in new situations and over time realized he really liked her and quit trying to impress her with his every word.

She slowly took to him as well. He was always polite and his constant references to talking to God eventually ceased to concern her and became an amusement instead. She began to see it as just an adorable quirk. She found it ironic that a man who is on intimate terms with the Almighty, kills other men, and keeps company with a whore. When she quit working her trade and assumed ownership of the cantina, she only slept with one man— Jack. He became a good lover in his own right. She enjoyed her place in an exclusive relationship.

Now she had just been slapped in the face with a crude and clumsy breakup from a man who finally wants the married life…but with another woman. He had not said as much, but she knew it was her past that was the reason for his leaving. In fact, he had always been adamant before that her past was not an issue when it would come up in one of their conversations, but that was a lie. It always is. When a man says something is not a reason, it is usually the only reason.

She had shown him many hours of pleasure that she doubted another woman could emulate, so she knew his wanting another woman could not be based on sex. The only possible answer had to be perceived "respectability." Men fall in love with their whores all the time, but only as far as wanting to be in bed where the relationship began. In their mind's eye, they confuse "being in love with her" with "being in love with having sex with her". A man may want a whore in his bedroom, but not on his arm.

"Lass, I do love you in my own way, but this happened suddenly. I didn't see it comin', I swear. She and her family are good simple folk and were gettin' a bad deal from the government so I went to see the president and in return for his favor, I promised to do this job for him. I think that's fair. But I didn't set out to hurt you, I swear, and that shit about your past is nonsense. People do what they have to in order to survive. You're a smart business woman and now you run the place, so what's wrong with that, I'm askin'? Besides, with my background, I ain't got the right to be sayin' what's proper, for Christ's sakes."

She had tears in her eyes as she reached her hand across the table and said, "Take care of yourself menso but for a while, when you are nearby, do not stop to see me…please. This is going to take some time to get over."

"Delia, I am sorry; believe me. I know you don't want to be hearin' it just now, but if you ever need me for anything, just get word to me and I'll come chargin'!" he said trying to convince himself that somehow the last sentence was a noble offer of continued friendship. Thinking his feeble attempt at sincerity had somehow allowed him the high ground; he kissed her hand and left the cantina.

As they mounted, one of the men told of hearing about a dangerous gang of bandits with a hideout in a large cave just a few miles down the road towards Chihuahua.

Jack, grateful for the opportunity to get his mind on something other than his guilt over hurting the feelings of a special woman shouted, "Well lads, let's go earn today's peso. They ain't payin' us to just look pretty you know."

When they were within two miles of the bandit's hideout, Jack signaled a halt. He said, "Look lads, I've got an old friend, a Cheyenne tracker named Stands Among Men who said to kill as many of your enemy as you can before they even know they are in a war, so that's what we're goin' to do by god. At first light, I'll blow the head off any lookouts with this," he patted his Sharps," and Hector here will toss a couple of sticks of his trusty dynamite into the cave's mouth and the rest of you will kill every som-bitch that tries to scramble out. When all hell breaks out, whoever is the closest will spook their horses so if any of them do make it outside, they'll be walkin'. No campfires tonight and no noise. Remember our strength is we're a bunch of sneaky bastards, so act like it."

Just before daylight, Jack nodded to Hector to light the fuse of a bundle of dynamite sticks and aimed his rifle at the lookout who was dozing with his back against a boulder several yards from the mouth of the cave. The man paid dearly for that laxness and the battle was on. Hector galloped up and tossed his bundle into the opening and fled back to a safe distance. The explosion killed all but three bandits who died as they staggered out of the cave profoundly dazed.

Thick smoke choked the air and mangled and dismembered bodies lay all about. The carnage would have sickened a normal man, but to Jack and his men it was a point of pride. A group of vicious men had been dispatched in a most gruesome manner and all was as it should be.

A grinning Jack playfully punched Hector on the shoulder and said, "Lad that shit is somethin', I'm sayin'! Remind me not to rile you none, but next time leave the rest of us somethin' to do goddamn it! We got all dressed up too, don't you see?"

Hector Montez surveyed the results of his work with something akin to professional pride for a job well done. He was the "explosives" man do to his experience with dynamite used in his career of robbing banks by blowing their safes. He came to the rurales when his last bank job resulted in an excessive explosion that brought the entire bank down upon his head. President Diaz, himself, commuted his prison sentence if he agreed to join this new strike force. Looking about him at the destruction his expertise had wrought, he thought, "Damn, I'm good!" It was the first time he had ever used dynamite to end a life and was pleased with the results. He was not in the least perturbed with the human toll. He was no stranger to killing having done it several times in shootouts, but had never used explosives and was impressed at the lethality of the weapon.

Jack turned a blind eye as the men rifled the bodies for valuables reasoning they were not exactly getting rich in the rurales. He figured it was natural for men who had once been bandits themselves. He had them roundup the horses to give to poor farmers and villagers in the area. The final count was eighteen dead and not even a scratch on his men. He announced, "I'm as proud as hell of you lads. My only rule is to keep shootin' until they quit shootin' back and if you're still breathin' when the noise stops, you've done good! Goddamn it you done it like proper Irish heathens, I'm tellin'. This ought to send the message we want sent, you reckon?"

The message was sent and received. Over the next month, they had three more similar incidents with no causalities of their own and twenty bandits dead. Activity noticeably dropped off well enough for Jack and his men to return to the Garcia farm for some unfinished business.

Chapter Sixteen

On his wedding day, Jack's stomach was a pit of burning embers. Besides the usual nervousness of a groom, he was concerned because word had gotten out and the assembling crowd was much larger than he had cared for it to be. Notice of the wedding had been spread by word of mouth and he felt that possibly in the crowd of villagers and neighboring haciendas there may be a relative of someone he had dispatched.

The day before the wedding, the priest had made Jack come to the church for confession. He had been born a Catholic but had not been inside a church since the day he arrived in America. Reyes accompanied him to the church and when he entered the confessional, the older man muttered to himself, "This will probably take hundreds of 'Hail Mary's' and 'Our Father's' for his penance."

Jack knelt and crossed himself and began, "Bless me father for I have sinned. It has been...twenty-five years since my last confession, yeah, that's right, about twenty-five years. Sorry. I went to church the first day I got to America and kinda forgot to go back," he added sheepishly.

"Well, you're here now and that's what matters. God is always ready to accept you back my son, so come to Him and share what is in your heart. But you don't have to tell me everything you have done in all of those years; just what you think is important. I have somewhere to be in a few days," the priest teased.

Jack spent the next quarter hour unburdening his heart. Of all the deaths he had caused, he felt guilt in only a few of them; those he killed from a distance and who had absolutely no idea their last judgment was at hand. Most had been confronted face to face and they had their chance to either defend themselves or flee. In his mind, that absolved him from guilt for those who had chosen unwisely, at least they had been warned.

One particular point affected him greatly. When he first settled at the O'Brian's ranch, he sent a letter to his parents telling of his safe arrival. His uncle wrote in return and told of their untimely deaths. He never wrote back to the man acknowledging his letter. For some reason, that rudeness suddenly bothered him.

He told of "impure thoughts" for Carolina but conveniently omitted "lust" for Anna. He figured since he was marrying her, it didn't count. In fact, he conveniently omitted a large portion of his major sins.

The old priest was relieved that it was finally at an end. He absolved him, gave him his penance and said that he would see him tomorrow at the wedding. He smiled that God must surely love that man, or else why had He let him live such a long and violent life?

During the wedding itself, Jack was on his knees in front of the priest with his back to the congregation for what seemed like hours. He kept thinking that at least he was in the right place if it was time to meet his maker. This was the first time in his adult life he had been in a large group of people unarmed, and he couldn't possibly have ever turned his back on such a mob before. He just hoped his men were paying attention.

As they walked from the church, she turned to him and asked, "What were you grinning about during the service?"

He smiled, "I was lookin' at Christ on the Cross and said 'Lad, if you get me out of this alive, I'll owe you one.'"

"What does that mean?" she demanded, "Get you out of our wedding?" She was furious until he quit laughing long enough to answer, "No sweetheart. I was on my knees with my back to everybody and not a gun to my name! I just knew I was goin' to get meet Himself before we got to the 'I do's.' I was just trying to make a deal's all."

She stopped on the church steps and gave him a tender look and whispered, "You Irish heathen, you don't make deals with God!"

"Want to bet?" he winked, "been doin' it all my life. Got you, didn't I?"

"I'll remind you of that someday when you start to think I was sent from hell! We'll see what you think of your little deal with God then," she laughed.

"Let me remind you of how I take care of my mistakes," he winked.

Later that day the couple got a surprise. A local government official had wired the capital with the news which was his normal job of providing any information of interest in his area. The president heard of it and sent the couple a congratulatory telegram. But the biggest surprise of all was three days later several wagons of building materials showed up at the farm and workers set to building a large house worthy of a hacienda. It was accompanied by a message of thanks for the job well done and it was hoped that he accept this gift from his "great friend in the Palace". Included was the deed of ownership for the five hundred acres surrounding the farm's meager existing twenty. Even though it was in Jack's name, he told his father-in-law that it was the Garcia hacienda and he still considered himself a guest and not the owner.

1878 had turned out to be a very good year for Jack and his new bride. He had gone from a dubious US marshal to a prominent Mexican citizen landowner and the captain of a special rurale strike force. He put his arms around a tearful Anna and said, "Not bad for a poor Irish boy who once ate grass to survive, I'm thinkin'."

* * * *

Jack rode up the government offices and was met at the steps by a rather effeminate lieutenant who said, "Captain Rose, will you follow me please. I am Lt. de Valencia; I am an aide to Colonel Huerta. His offices are just this way." Jack was amused at the prancing aide and tried not to laugh at his prissy ways.

He had been summoned by Huerta and almost did not come, but his curiosity got the best of him. Hector and the men wanted to accompany him but he insisted that he could handle anything that backstabbing rat could throw at him. He promised his men that he would keep a wary eye towards events and if something went wrong, Huerta would not live through it either. He laughed when Hector said that if it was a trap and he didn't survive, Huerta and nobody in his family would either, including his mother's cat.

Jack was shown into an ornately appointed office crammed full of oversized and overstuffed leather furniture. Even the massive oaken desk in the center was twice as large as any he had ever seen. He grinned as he wondered who decorated this "whorehouse?" It sure as hell wasn't a man's office!

The aide indicated which chair for Jack to sit in, and silently left the room. Huerta kept reading papers from the stack in front of him for several seconds before he looked up and acknowledged Jack's arrival. He was being purposefully rude in order to watch Jack's reaction. Seeing that Jack had a slightly bemused smile tug at the corners of his mouth, Huerta spoke, "I'm so glad you could find the time to see me. I know your duties must keep you very busy indeed."

Jack smiled and said, "It is my pleasure. We ain't so swamped that I couldn't rush right down here lickity-split. I've got lots of time now since there seems to be a lot fewer bad guys than there was here-awhile-back. So what'cha need?"

Huerta was not used to having to deal with such a flippant attitude and said in a stern manner, "Do you know a Carlos Murrieta?"

"You mean the 'late Carlos Murrieta' don't you? 'Cause from what I hear, the lad ain't among us no more. That happens sometimes when you have twenty horses that ain't yours and you'd rather argue about it than explain how it happened, I'm supposin'."

"Then you admit it?"

"Admit what?"

"That you executed him and his men!"

Jack laughed out loud and angered Huerta even further and said, "Well the way I heard it works is that at an execution, the guest of honor don't get to shoot first which is what they done as soon as we came into view. I'd call it more like committin' suicide myself. Why the interest in a two-bit horse thief and his boyos?"

Huerta was livid at this point and shouted, "Carlos Murrieta was my wife's nephew! He was the son of her sister and brother-in-law, and they are a very respectable family of great prominence!"

"If by 'prominence' you mean successful bandits, then you're on to somethin' there lad. They stole every blade of grass on that entire ranch and what grazes on it. But nobody ever did anythin' about it since rumor had it that they had some sort of guardian angel somewhere, and I'll be a two-tailed cat if it ain't so after all!"

Huerta shouted, "I've got you now Senor Gringo Gunslinger! I have warrants for the arrest of you and your men!" As he reached for the bell on his desk, Jack said icily, "If you ring that goddamned bell, you won't be here to see if anyone answers!"

"Are you threatening me?"

Jack stood and snarled, "Hell yes I'm threatenin' you! You need me to speak slower so you can keep up? I figured you'd start some shit, so I've got some lads outside and if I don't come out all smiles and such in a few minutes, they'll come stormin' in and I'll bet a blind three-legged dog would have a better chance of catchin' a jackrabbit than these butterflies of yours would have of doin' somethin' about it!" He was bluffing but Huerta would not know that. He was relying on his obvious anger and reputation to be convincing. It worked because Huerta dismissed him with a warning that next time they met it may go differently.

Jack countered with, "I just might go over to the president's office and let you explain to him what you got on your mind, you som-bitch!"

With that, he left and thought to himself that Hector will be tickled to learn that he was right in his warnings. He decided that the next time he has dealings with that rat Huerta he'll take Hector's advice and show up with the lads.

Chapter Seventeen

Carolina was attending to the purchase of supplies at the market when a barefooted peasant approached with hat in hand and asked if she could spare a few centavos. She smiled and said that there was not much he could buy for a few centavos so she gave the man five pesos instead. The stunned man bowed several times as he backed away repeating, "God will bless you senorita." He said it at least a half dozen times before he was far enough away to politely stop. She thought to herself that her station in life was indeed a blessing when compared to that of the man she had just met. Her heart went out to him and those like him. She thought of how their numbers seemed to be increasing daily. There was a time when there were only two or three peasants on each block begging for whatever could be coaxed from passers-by, but now there were dozens, especially in front of the churches where people feeling good about their spirituality were most likely to share.

Another stranger, only marginally better dressed, was watching from a distance and thinking what she had just done gracious and noble, presented himself. Feeling suddenly charitable, she reached for something to give to the new man. He declined the offer saying, "Gracias senorita but no, that is not why I approached you. I saw what you did for that stranger to you. You must be a compassionate woman, to care for the plight of a fellow human being. God will smile on you."

"Thank you my friend, but as you can see, he already has." she answered.

As he stood there, he couldn't help but notice the fine horse and carriage as well as Carolina's nice clothes. He then continued, "It would seem that it is true. You have been blessed many times, and since you are a good and caring woman, maybe you would like to come to a meeting tonight. There are many, many men like the one you just helped."

Carolina, a natural skeptic asked, "Just what kind of meeting senor?"

"It is the kind of meeting where good men commit to helping other men in need. There are many hundreds of the poor who were once able to feed their families before the programs of President Diaz cost them all."

"Senor, I don't know you and after I have listened to you, I don't want to be seen talking to you. It is people like you who get people like me in trouble. You place my family in danger because you talk of a meeting that will cost you your life if the wrong men see you. You're talking treason."

"No senorita, we are talking of helping the poor only. We seek to find a good and much respected person to present our concerns to the president. Someone such as you would have a better chance to see the president than would we. We merely wish to beg for relief and present our point of view and hope someone like you will do this for us, nothing more, I swear. Angry men make themselves known in newspaper articles and speeches of open revolt, but we are not like that. We seek peaceful understanding from the government, and that is where someone of your stature can be of help."

"No sir, you are looking for a fool, for that's what someone would have to be to present a list of treasonous demands to a man like the president. He has the power to execute you for such! He has done nothing to me, in fact my family has benefited greatly from his policies. I am sorry that you obviously have not done as well, but there is nothing I can do. There it is."

"I'm sorry to have bothered you senorita. It was my mistake, please forgive me. Goodbye." With that he disappeared up a side street.

Carolina and Tony were sitting on the veranda having their morning coffee when a rider approached. He was well dressed in a tailored military uniform. He waited at the hitching post as he asked permission to approach. Receiving a positive answer, he dismounted, tied his horse and climbed the steps to where they sit.

He removed his sombrero and said, "Senor and senorita, good morning. My name is Lt. Gustavo Ruiz. I work for the government in the capital and I have been assigned to the town of San Tomas. I have some likenesses for you to look at." He spread three photographs in front of them and asked, "Do you know any of these men?"

Tony said, "They look a lot like pictures on Wanted Posters."

Ruiz said, "They are of sorts. Have you ever seen these men?"

Carolina looked briefly and said, "This one I've seen in San Tomas. He talked to me on the street for a minute, but I don't know his name."

"His name is Carlos Constanzo. What did he want?"

"He babbled some nonsense about coming to a meeting."

"What kind of meeting, senorita?"

"The kind of meeting that gets men like you to come to my home wanting to ask questions. I told him I didn't want anything to do with him or his meeting. He said he was sorry and left. I haven't seen him again, nor had I better."

"That was wise. It agrees with the report I received of the incident. Tell me senor Salcido, have you ever seen any of these men yourself?"

"I have never seen him nor have I ever seen the other two. What have they done?"

"They are fomenting unrest. They are forming subversive groups from outlawed trade unions and other radical elements.

They are signing petitions demanding the resignation of His Excellency, The President. There has even been talk of what actions should be taken if he refuses. They are in violation of the new decree banning political speech. When Constanzo talked to you that day, he was only dangerously close to sedition. They have persisted, and since the new decree, they have reached the level of treason. I should be careful if I were you and avoid these men in the future."

With that, Ruiz rose and with an exaggerated flourish with his sombrero, he bade them good-day and rode off towards San Tomas leaving the pair stunned over what had just taken place. After several minutes, Carolina said in somber tones, "You know what this means, don't you?"

"Yes, it means that there are spies everywhere. They even watched you the other day when you were in town and not aware of them. For the time being it would be wise to avoid those who are unknown to us. You never know who is watching, or what they have on their mind. People like us are probably not the target of their investigations. We are not the kind of people who are writing seditious petitions or complaining of the government's programs. In fact, these people know we benefit greatly from the government's policies, and they know that we know too. So I think the reason for today's visit was merely to let us know they are there and watching. If the generals really feared those men he asked about, they would be in a prison this very minute. That is the lesson we must take away from this, we must be cautious. We must lead our lives as normal as we can, but we must be cautious."

They found themselves in the odd position of trying to lead as normal a life as possible, but at the same time the heightened awareness of their surroundings made their lives anything but normal. They avoided strangers, and refused to talk politics with even the oldest of their friends. Tony even approached Nettie with the idea of having Juana on the ranch might draw unwanted attention given her background as a runaway displaced person. Nettie countered that the woman never even left the house except for church and if the government was afraid of a poor destitute and defenseless old Indian woman, then things were indeed worse than they appeared. Tony gave in on this point, which was usual when his wife made sense, and the subject never came up again.

Eventually things returned to normal. Nothing more came from the visit by the authorities and over time it was learned the three suspects had been arrested and transferred to the capital and were not heard from again.

Things were actually better than normal. The extra profits were plowed back into the hacienda. Better brood-stock was purchased and more wranglers were hired. The export of his horses to Europe increased, generating yet even more profits. This was facilitated by the building of new railroads in the area with a spur adjacent to the ranch, an acknowledgement to Tony from his longtime friend. As far as Tony's operation was concerned, the president's policies seemed to be written with him specifically in mind. His ranch was the showplace for Positivism. The list of Diaz partisans reflected the Salcido clan.

Chapter Eighteen

Jack had a compound built at the front gate for his men. They were bivouacked at the Juarez garrison some ten miles away during construction. His friend Alvaro Silva gave him a good ribbing about out ranking Jack now that he was a rurale, but Jack countered with the comment of what the good colonel could kiss.

A report came in that there were several professional gunmen in San Tomas. Jack and his men rode there to investigate. Jack entered the square and saw three men sitting on the wall of the fountain. He galloped straight for them. He leapt from the saddle as the horse slid to a halt. It had the desired effect. The three men froze and failed to fan out as they had planned. The man on the left tried to step to his right but Jack cut him off, "That's good where you are. You wouldn't be thinkin' of spreadin' out now would you lad? I'm gettin' old and don't see so well anymore, so I need you to remain in a wad like, if you please." He looked closely at the three, none of which could have been much older than twenty. "Hell, maybe I am gettin' old after all," he thought to himself. They were all fresh-faced American boys none of which he knew so he asked, "What is this all about lads? Did I shoot one of your daddies? Or maybe I covered one of your mommas? Which was it?"

The man in the center did not take the bait and remained calm, "No Mr. Rose, we had nothing to do, so we decided to look you up. But it seems that you've gotten so old, you need your army with you."

Jack snarled, "Don't be worryin' about the lads, but that nasty lookin' som-bitch is Hector and he loves me and there ain't no tellin' what he might do." Hector puckered his lips and made a kissing movement.

"We wanted to see if you were as good as they say," the man in the center said.

"Well lad, it seems we are all about to find out. Any last words in case I am?"

"Yeah, you're an arrogant bastard!" the man on the right shouted as he drew.

For some reason Theo Johns' words came rushing into his head as he reached for his gun, "Accuracy is more important than speed." That proved prophetic as the man's shot was wide and he died never knowing he had out drawn Fast Jack Rose. The second man's gun was just then clearing leather when a bullet ripped into his heart, but the third man hit Jack in his side, spinning him around. As the shooter came back into view, Jack squeezed off two quick shots, both hitting him in the chest.

He dropped to his knees, more from relief than from the pain in his side. It was over, three men were dead and he was still alive. For the first time he had felt the bullet's bite and knew it was just a matter of time before another fast gun would repeat what had just happened, but fatally. He had been outdrawn but the man missed with his shot and odds were not in his favor to survive by such luck again. He had just experienced the reason so few gunmen live long enough to retire. He was starting to feel each of his thirty-six years, and for the first time in his adult life considered walking away. That idea would prove fleeting for as the sounds of the awed crowd made their way into his conscious mind, his arrogance was again stoked and he was the same Fast Jack Rose of famed lethality.

A large group of people joined his men and came running to him having witnessed the most exciting event ever in their lives. They had seen a man of legendary reputation kill three gringo pistol-fighters enhancing that reputation even more. His men had only seen his accuracy with a rifle but were in stunned disbelief at the speed of the man they called "El Capitan Jack". As far as the locals were concerned, he may have been born elsewhere, but he was now a man of San Tomas.

One of the first to reach him was the local doctor. He took a quick look at the wound and was relieved. He told Jack the bullet merely dug a trench in the flesh as it passed through and hadn't hit any organs. He said it would probably not bleed much but it would awfully painful for a few days.

While the doctor bandaged the wound, Jack looked at his torn and bloody shirt and asked if someone could bring him a new one. He said he at least wanted to get into the house before his wife killed him. He laughed that she would do what the three dead men failed to do.

*   *   *   *

A few days later and hundreds of miles away, Lt. Gustavo Ruiz approached headquarters to make his latest report on the town of San Tomas. He entered the office of his superior and congratulated him for recently being promoted to General. They exchanged salutes and Ruiz began, "Mi general, San Tomas has become infested with subversives. They run the gamut from disloyal generals displeased with what they see as their cut of the spoils of the old regime to disposed campesinos and radicals. All of them voice displeasure at the growing power of the state apparatus. They demand more of a voice in a true democracy. With the added pressure the rurales have put on the city of Chihuahua, they have spread to all of the other towns in the state. They especially express complaints that the rurales are not a constabulary for their protection but strike breaking anti-union thugs instead. They say the rurales are reluctant to confront the robber-Capitans and other rural unrest but would rather break the skulls of peasants demanding equality. The most damning is the newspaper account of President Diaz saying 'shoot them all' in reply to Veracruz governor Luis Mien Y Teran's telegram asking for instructions in dealing with the nine businessmen accused of sedition."

Taking a sip of water for his throat, he continued, "They no longer attempt at keeping their meetings secret, but we have made a few arrests. The list of the ringleaders is in this dossier." He slid the folder across the desk.

Huerta read the dossier closely and asked, "What is this entry on Jack Rose? It says he killed three men in the town square. What was done about it?"

"Done? Nothing was done sir. In the first place, he is a captain of the special independent rurale unit separate from the other contingent in the complaint. There were a hundred witnesses, including the local police, and myself as well who saw the three men start the fight."

"I know his assignment, but you say they started it?"

"Yes sir, you should have seen it. Three gringo gunfighters called him out, he rode up and faced them. One of them even drew first...he killed all three as quick as a man can blink! It was magnificent! I have never seen the like!"

Huerta started to get annoyed, "Never mind about that, what have you found out about this man? I know he works for President Diaz, but where do his loyalties really lay? Is he what he seems?"

"He is a Diaz man and loudly so, my general. The spy we have inside the hacienda says none of the family has ever hinted anything but extreme loyalty, most especially him. But this would be natural for a man appointed by the president himself. Sir, why do you ask?"

"Thank you for your report," Huerta said ignoring the question. "I'll read it thoroughly later, but for now take two days off and see your family. Then return to your post and continue to keep a close eye on the developments there. By the end of next week a detachment of soldiers will arrive to escort prisoners back here for public trials. Make more arrests; we are going to put an end to that hotbed of insurrection. Good luck and dismissed." The men exchanged salutes again, and Ruiz left the office.

Later that night in bed with his wife, Ruiz confided, "Something is going on. I made my report to Huerta about the growing subversion by radical elements in San Tomas, yet all he was interested in was a local gunfighter. That was very odd."

Gustavo Ruiz was the son and grandson of honored military men. All he had ever known was the army. He was disciplined and loyal to a fault and considered orders from superiors as "the word of God". He married Maria Perez, his childhood sweetheart and the only woman he ever kissed, the day he graduated from the academy. Thinking military life too harsh and unstable for his delicate and sickly wife, he insisted that she remain at her family's estate near Mexico City where she would be properly cared for. He was considerate to a fault. He missed being with her, but it was a necessary sacrifice for her welfare. Originally, he had hoped to be assigned to the capitol to be near her, but his postings seemed to be as far away as possible. He never actually asked for a transfer for fear that he would seem disgruntled with his assignments, so he took the phrase in step that every army on earth uses when it orders a man to distant places, "For the needs of the service." As a trained artillery officer with high marks at the academy, he was vastly disappointed when these needs turned out to be a gatherer of gossip, and a peeper at keyholes.

His wife studied her husband for a minute. He was very smart and a good man, very loyal to his superiors and the army, yet he senses something may not be as it should. She asked, "What do you think it means my husband? It would seem that obviously this man intrigues him. Maybe it is because this man is dangerous that he is fascinating."

"You should have seen it Maria. He was a gunfighter from Texas and now a rurale captain. This man faced three. One man had already drawn his gun and fired when he drew and shot him, he then quickly turned to the second who was pulling his gun at the same time and killed him. The third man fired, wounding this man who spun around and hit him twice in the chest. It all over just this quick," he snapped his fingers to show his wife the speed. "Three men were dead and the smoke from the guns still hung in the air. I knew these men faced danger, but I would never have imagined what that danger looked like. It was magnificent! I just pray I never have to face a man like that. I would not even try to match such courage."

She said in response, "Men like you do not have gunfights, so I shouldn't worry. Maybe Huerta only wanted to hear the story of this man. Maybe he admires such men."

"Maybe...but he seems distant like he is watching everything and everyone a little too closely. I cannot tell exactly what I see from him, but it is there if only I could sort through it. But it is for another day, I'm tired so let us sleep."

Ruiz had no way of knowing, but his instincts were sound. Of all the men gathering under the growing thunderclouds of inevitable revolution, Victoriano Huerta should have been scrutinized closer than any other man...regardless of side.

Chapter Nineteen

Reyes was riding his property when his horse was shot from under him. The air exploded with the sound of rifle fire, but oddly, none of the shots actually landed close enough to threaten him. It was as if the shooters were trying to pin him down, but not kill him. Balled up behind the dead animal for protection, he returned fire. The assailants were hopelessly out of range of the feeble offerings from his pistol.

Jack and two of his men heard the sound of gunfire and charged over the hill into a wall of flying lead. Jack was knocked from his horse with a bullet to his left shoulder. He landed hard dislocating that same shoulder as well. Reyes screamed his name and started to crawl towards his stricken son-in-law, oblivious of the battle. It took another few seconds before he realized that the shooting had stopped. He could see the assailants fleeing in the distance. He instantly knew that Jack had been the target all along. They had shot at him to only lure Jack into an ambush. When Jack had fallen from his horse, they assumed he was dead and their work finished.

Reyes was busy trying to staunch the flow of blood while his men chased down and apprehended the two assailants within minutes. Jack was fortunate because the bullet had hit him a glancing blow on the fleshy part of his left shoulder above the collarbone. No bones were broken. He lost only a little blood, and the wound didn't appear to be serious. Hector had arrived by the time he came to. He helped Jack on his horse and assisted him to the house. A doctor was sent for.

While everyone fretted, Anna walked to where he sat and satisfied that he still had his senses, said in a matter-of-fact tone, "He'll be fine. My man is too mean to die from only one bullet! He's Irish you know. You can hang one, but if you're going to shoot one, you better bring more than one bullet!"

Within minutes of the doctor's leaving, he was bellowing more about the pain in his reset shoulder than the gunshot wound. "Goddamn it woman, how did I manage to dislocate my god...shoulder?"

"Because my darling husband," she started, "you are not smart enough to fall in a sensible manner. If you had landed on your head, you would have been just fine."

"Has anyone ever told you just how funny you are?"

"Yes, many times."

"I doubt it! My darlin' wife, when my shoulder heals, I'm going to beat you!"

"Now that I doubt!" she countered.

Later that evening with his left arm in a sling, he went to the compound to interrogate the prisoners. Their faces were bruised and bloody from the obvious beating given them by Hector and Nacio, another of Jack's men devoid of social graces.

"Lads, what's this about? Who hired you?" Jack asked.

"Kiss my ass you bastard!" one snapped.

"Nacio, you want to ask him?"

Nacio walked up and shot him in the forehead. He then looked at the other prisoner who started shouting, "Shafer! Judge Shafer hired us, I swear!"

Jack smiled and said to Nacho, "Interesting technique. How'd it come to you?"

"It is an old method when one is too stupid mean to want to talk. It encourages others to cooperate, like this moricon," he answered.

Jack nodded his head, "I must remember that. I'll be a two-headed yellow spider if that ain't the damndest thing I ever saw!"

He then turned to the remaining prisoner and said, "Are you absolutely sure Judge Bob Shafer hired you to kill me. It is very important lad. Describe him. What did he look and sound like?"

He listened to the man's description of Shafer and agreed that he had it right. He was especially angered when he heard the judge had paid them one thousand dollars each for the murder. He shouted, "That cheap som-bitch! He'd steal money from me just to use it later to have my ass killed! What do you think of that Hector?"

Hector grinned and said, "I think he needs a visit mi Capitan. Tell me who this Shafer is and where to find him, and I'll take the heads of these two bavoso's to him in a bag. Then I will bring his head back to you."

Jack laughed for several seconds and then said, "No my friend. I appreciate the offer, but the last face he sees on this earth is to be mine, I'm thinkin' God demands it'''.

The next morning he was in the alley behind the courthouse in El Paso, waiting for the judge's buggy to appear. Soon the judge rounded the corner in his rig. As he alit, Jack stepped into view and snarled, "Surprise you bastard!"

"Jack!" he blurted his legs barely able to support his weight.

"You're goddamned right, alive and well, no thanks to you!"

"I'm sorry Jack, there was nothing personal," he started.

Jack interrupted, "Nothin' personal? The next time you get shot, think about how personal that was!"

"I was just tying up loose ends. It was business," he stammered.

"Loose ends? I'm a loose end?"

"Yes and I'm sorry, but I've been appointed to the federal court in Washington and I was afraid our relationship would come to light. How would it look if they found out that I had given you a license to kill? That means everyone who ended up dead could be laid at my door too. That wouldn't do. I'm a judge for Christ's sakes! I'm supposed to believe in the law and not ordering the death of men before they can even stand trial. I love you like a son Jack, but I was afraid that one day you may say something causally and it would come out. I'm not as strong as you so I panicked. But I see now that I was thinking wrong. I made a mistake and I now realize that you ain't the kind to go blabbing for no reason. You can keep a secret, I know that now. Maybe we can still work together like before. How about it Jack? Can you forgive me? "

The look of total terror in his eyes started to slowly abate. He had angered the most dangerous man in two countries but was emboldened because he was still alive. The Jack Rose he knows would shoot first and sort it out later, but since he hadn't yet shot, the judge grasped at the hope he could still reason with him; he continued in his belief that he was safe.

Jack, meanwhile, had imperceptibly inched closer to the judge cutting down the distance between the two. As he got close enough to smell the judge's sweat he said, "Forgive you? Forgive the man who tried to have me killed where I live so my wife would be seein' me die?"

The judge grasping for any opening said, "You can't shoot me, everyone will hear the shot."

"Yeah, but they won't hear this," with that he brandished the knife he had been hiding behind his back and slit the judge's throat. He stepped back as the man lost consciousness, fell forward and died. He wiped the blood off the knife on the judge's suit coat, put it back in its scabbard and rode for home. He passed several people on the streets but didn't care if they recognized him. He wouldn't be back and the law couldn't touch him where he was going. He was no longer a Texan, in his mind he was now completely Mexican. A red-headed, freckled faced Mexican with an Irish brogue, but Mexican all the same—and he had the papers to prove it!

Upon arriving home he was amused to hear that the other prisoner was shot trying to escape. He laughed while Hector described Nacio's miraculous shot hitting the man between the eyes while he was fleeing the other way. He remembered the judge's phrase, "tying up loose ends" and thought how appropriate. He then asked Hector if he had found the "blood money" on the prisoners and was told they had nothing on them. He laughed and said to make sure the other men got their share of "nothing" too.

Part III
The Second Act

Chapter Twenty

The 1880's were eventful for the regime of President Porfirio Diaz. He had stepped down after his first term as he had promised with his strict adherence to the constitutional "No Re-election" policy. He had often warned of a possible dictatorship if men were allowed to stay in power without an effective means for change. When the regime of his handpicked successor, Manuel Gonzalez proved ineffectual and corrupt, he took back the Presidency in 1884 which he would hold until 1911 through intimidation and violence, ironically becoming the very dictator he had warned about years earlier.

He put the country on the gold standard as he made the peso one of soundest currencies in the world. He created an excellent banking system, and an effective system of tax collection. He abolished state tariffs, taxes on production, sales taxes, and he balanced the budget. His economy raced forward as he procured increased foreign capital. He encouraged the building of roads, factories, dams, industries and better modern farms all of which made him loved by millions of middle class Mexicans. Unfortunately, most of these advancements came at the expense of the working class, farmers and peasants thus making him hated by millions of other Mexicans.

These same 1880's were very good for the Salcido household as well. Tony doubled his holdings as the hacienda became the best run and one of most profitable in the history of the country worth in the millions, rivaling that of the Terrazas clan of Chihuahua. Sadly, in 1886 his beloved Nettie died in her sleep at the age of 66. A good and descent woman was gone. She did not suffer.

That year also saw another tragedy befall the Salcido family when Ricardo was shot in the back, murdered for his wallet and watch by bandits in Chihuahua as he rode home from the bank where he and his brother Roberto worked. Being twins, they had spent their entire life together and sought the same career and they even chose the same bank. He was thirty-one. The loss of both was devastating for Tony. He was as a rudderless ship before the wind. He didn't even have any grandchildren to lean on. He had hoped Carolina would marry and present him with a houseful of grandchildren, but that was not to be. After the family learned the disappointing news of Jack's marriage, she lost interest in men altogether. In the years since, she went into a shell and focused on the family business to the exclusion of a personal life.

Tony died on the first day of May, 1889. He had lived sixty-nine productive and prosperous years. He had lived a decade longer than any of his long time friends and nearly twice the average for men of the time. He was much loved by his two remaining children, household staff, employees, and by the community at large. The size of his funeral proved that. The proletariat was best represented but the aristocracy and even the peasant class was in attendance in noticeable numbers. The priest was pleased by the turnout and during the service pointed out that Tony would be much missed.

The day he left the seminary, he bought one stallion and four brood mares and in thirty years had turned it into worldwide concern. His daughter now continued the hacienda's growth. She had spent the last years of her father's life learning the operation in preparation for just this eventuality. She had been born to it. She was more than capable, she was dynamic.

As 1890 dawned, she took stock of her life. She was a stunningly beautiful thirty-four year old woman. She still turned heads when out in public, not that she was interested.

Her first year as haciendada had been fulfilling, if tiring. She had to oversee all phases of the operation. She had always, more or less, held the same political views as her father. The family had grown into wealth, and had lived very comfortably. Families like hers benefited the most from Diaz's programs and owed their allegiance to his government. But over time, she could not help but notice that the gap between those of means and those without was widening at an alarming rate. She instinctively understood that the real barometer of a nation's health was the condition of its poor and disenfranchised; more to the point; the level of caring by the government for the predicament of these people was an indicator of the possible life-span of the regime. When a man is unable to feed his family, he is open to the ideas of other men, especially impatient and insistent men. She was becoming more conflicted as her awareness of the dilemma of the poor increased. Being human, of course her heart went out to these people, but as the person responsible for the welfare of three dozen employees and their families her first concern was for her holdings. These impatient and insistent men more and more railed against people like her. The irony was not lost on her; she employed people and paid them well, but for some bizarre reason that made her an example of those who oppressed the people. It was the type of circular argument that was nonsense on the face of it, but appealed to less intelligent and easily swayed portion of malcontents it was targeted at.

As in all human confrontational situations, it was all about assigning blame. Someone was at risk so someone else must be at fault. Someone should be made to answer for the injustice and who better than those who obviously prospered under the status quo. She knew that the impatient and insistent men would someday convince desperate men that if they took up arms and stormed the Presidential Palace they could then settle accounts with people like her. That was all that was needed. It was simple really; men with no voice could find one at the end of a gun and people like her would have to listen.

For her, listening was not the issue. She was unable to speak. She made huge donations to the church for the benefit of the poor, but she could not let it be known since Diaz had spies everywhere. Her benevolence would have consequences because it was, in effect, aiding and abetting the enemy. To the men in power, she was not merely feeding the poor but she was assisting those who would wrest away their power. It was not true, but they believed it and that was enough.

It was not as though she would call attention to herself for doing what Christ had demanded of us all. She had too much dignity to boast, but the necessity for secrecy was compelling. Her conscience was clear that she was doing her Christian duty as her politics evolved to embrace the rightness of the cause of the "barefooted ones."

She feared the time when the disparate factions of men seeking action would be galvanized by a man of words. A smart man armed with weighty words is the most important constituent in any assembly. He is the one with the vision. He is the one with the capability to help other men see that vision. A truly great man of words has the capability to convince other men that the vision was theirs all along and that his words merely helped them see what they had already known. This great man of words has the capability to create desperation in those he would destroy. Try as he might, the desperate man would be unable to stay the hand for long of those who sought his destruction. When desperate men grasp with desperate hope at desperate solutions, impatient and insistent men soon have what they seek—rebellion. Insurrection would soon be encouraged by a man of words, a humble lawyer from Coahuila—Francisco Madero—a man feared by both Porfirio Diaz and Carolina Salcido, but for quite different reasons, yet, strangely for some of the same ones as well.

She stood and walked to the large windows and peered out over the valley and thought of how disorder was on the rise and every ranch in the area had become beset with theft...every ranch including hers. In a moment of nostalgic musings she thought to herself, "Well my darling Jack, where are you now that I need you? You scare the hell out of people who need it, and there are several around here that could use a good fright. Damn it! Why couldn't you have loved me instead of that ignorant peasant?" She then broke down and sobbed for hours. She had not cried over him in years, but she was lonely and the thought of the man she had loved since childhood in the arms of another was too much to bear.

*   *   *   *

Father Reynosa was giving the benediction as he dismissed mass in the church in the tiny village of San Angeles, in the Sierra Madre Occidental Mountains of Chihuahua. The village was isolated high in the mountains, and strangers were a rare sight so when two dozen armed men burst into the church it was a frightening event. The men lined the walls and ordered everyone to gather together in the center aisle.

A particularly evil looking man with piercing black eyes said, "My name is Guerrero, and I have killed more people than are in this church so listen well. If you do like I say, no-one will get hurt. There is a squad of rurales right behind me, and you are going to be my safe passage." Panic gripped the hostages and they began to scream. He became angered and fired his pistol in the air dislodging a piece of the ceiling as he shouted for quiet.

Jack and his men heard the shot as they entered the village. They had been on the trail of the bandit gang for several days. At the sound, they raced towards the church where they assumed the men were hiding owing to the inordinate number of horses tied there.

The rurales dismounted and took cover around the square facing the church. Jack stood in the center of the square and yelled for Guerrero to come out. After a few minutes, the bandit stood at the door with a pistol to the head of a small girl and shouted for Jack and his men to ride on or the child would die.

Jack said, "Lad, that's about the stupidest thing I've ever heard. If you shoot her, just how the hell are you goin' to get back inside? The only thing between you and hell is that little girl don't you see? If you kill her, I've got ten hateful som-bitches that'll blow your balls off by god!"

Guerrero snapped, "My men have twenty more hostages inside and they will kill them all cabrone!"

Jack laughed, "You just keep gettin' stupider by the minute! If you start shootin' folks you sure as hell won't have nothin' to hide behind then you dumb som-bitch! The only way you walk out still breathin' is to show your smiley faces and your empty hands." So why don't you be a good lad and go back inside and tell them mongrels to drop their guns and waltz out peaceable like. But of course, it's up to you."

"Are you not listening cabrone, if you don't leave this village, they will all die!"

"Look old son, they were dead the minute you rode into this goddamned place. That's God's doin's and I can't do anythin' about it, but I sure as hell can make you dread the day your daddy mounted your momma by god! And this I swear by all that's holy, if any of them good folks is harmed, you won't believe what happens next! My lads know more about pain than Satan! So throw them goddamned guns down and come on out. I've got better places to be, I'm tellin'."

Guerrero drug the girl back inside and shut the doors. After a few minutes, the doors opened back up and the bandits filed out with their hands in the air. They seemed to be unarmed except for the last man in line. He whipped out his pistol and aimed it at Jack. Nacio put a bullet in his ear before the man could get off a shot. Pandemonium broke out and several more were killed before the rest succeeded in halting the gunfire by waving their hands wildly above their heads. A quick search revealed six other men with concealed pistols.

Jack looked at Nacio and said, "Nice shot, lad. I'm glad you were payin' attention, I'm thinkin'."

Nacio grinned and said, "It was just too easy mi Capitan. Men like these do not give up without a fight so I kept my eye on them. I figured that if someone was going to do something it would be the last one. That's what I would have done if it was me."

"And right you were lad, right you were. I learned somethin' this day, by god, just shoot them all first and be done with it," he winked.

Father Reynosa began praying for the souls of the dead men when Jack said sarcastically for him to speak up; they were in hell now and probably could not hear him. Jack thought to himself that he would never understand priests. The dead men had just held their guns on his parishioners and threatened their death, yet here he was praying for the souls of these animals. He was just glad his own job did not require moral judgments, only resolute actions.

The priest said he would see to burying the dead, and Jack tied the hands of the rest and began to lead them to the compound in Juarez. He couldn't resist telling Guerrero that he hoped none of them "accidently" fell off their horses on the way down out of the mountains.

Chapter Twenty-One

The 1880's were eventful as well for the Garcia-Rose hacienda as Reyes demanded it be called. Even though Jack had had it registered with Reyes Garcia as the owner, he insisted it be changed to reflect both names. Jack protested but lost the argument.

Reyes had undergone something of a metamorphosis. For all of his life he had been a Benito Juarez partisan and a social liberal himself. He was for universal male suffrage including indigenous peoples and peasants. He advocated universal participation in the democratic process, but since Porfirio Diaz had presented him with his hacienda, he slowly became conflicted as to where his loyalties should lay. He could not in good conscience wish ill for his benefactor, but he could not dismiss his roots either. As a haciendada, he profited by Positivism for which he was grateful, but the loss of their holdings by the men who had been his life-long friends and neighbors caused him great anguish.

He never spoke of this to his son-in-law because he knew Jack's loyalties were firmly with his new friend, Diaz. He admired Jack's passions and would never have had a political discussion for fear of upsetting him. So he kept his opinions to himself, not even confiding in his daughter, for fear of putting pressure on her. She loved her husband and no doubt understood his point of view. He remained silent and put all of his energies and efforts in running his hacienda.

When Porfirio Diaz stepped down at the end of his term in 1880, Jack also resigned. He was smart enough to realize with a new man in the palace, he was no longer protected from the top. The new regime may not have the same tolerance for the way he did his job. It was a wise move because the term of office for the new president, Manuel Gonzalez, was strife ridden and political intrigue increased tenfold. No-one knew who to trust, so no-one was trusted. Reyes was relieved but remained silent.

The rurale post was dismantled and assimilated by the Juarez garrison. Jack had lobbied for it to remain on hacienda property but was denied by the new government. He had developed a genuine affection for his men, and he was most proud of the fact that in the nearly three years of their existence, he never lost a man. They had killed close to fifty bandits and arrested a like number, yet never had a man even seriously wounded.

The few head of cattle they began with three years earlier had grown to nearly one hundred head through normal reproduction but mostly additional purchases. It was quite a prosperous operation.

In 1884, upon Diaz's ouster of Gonzalez reclaiming the presidency, one of his first orders of business was a telegram to Jack asking him to rejoin his government. Jack wrote a thoughtful and apologetic letter respectfully declining the offer. Even though he was still only forty-two, he had lost his edge and no longer wanted any part of that life. He said he no longer felt able to tolerate days on end in a saddle with a gunfight at the end of the ride. God no longer required his services and his gun was no longer needed. He hoped the president would understand that he was content being a gentleman farmer, as he put it. He thanked the president again profusely for his gifts, and ended his letter.

Also in the same year, Sean Reyes Rose was born and named for his two grandfathers, but lived for only one month. Two years later another son was still-born.

The couple tried unsuccessfully for the next four years, and finally she became pregnant again. But Jack's world was shaken to its very core when his beloved Anna died in childbirth taking a daughter with her in March 1890. She was thirty-two. To his thinking, that was the final sign that God was done with him. He was devastated and went into virtual seclusion for weeks. He seldom talked and would sit for hours in a chair under the same tree he first kissed his precious Anna those many years earlier. Everyone was concerned but nobody intruded on his grief.

One day he was shaken back to reality when a messenger arrived with a letter from Carolina. She was at a hotel in Juarez and wished for him to come and see her. He was stunned and shouted to Reyes that he'd be back soon, saddled his horse and raced for Juarez.

He was nearly breathless when he reached her room. He stood for several seconds gaining composure before he knocked. When she called out for him to enter, all of his new found composure disappeared instantly as he almost tore the door from its hinges. They rushed to an embrace in the middle of the room. They held each other for minutes before she spoke, "I was sorry to read of your wife's death in the newspaper." He was surprised that it had made the papers in San Tomas until she said that anything concerning him was news for the townsfolk. They still considered him one of them. She told him of the deaths of her parents and brother.

He said, "I'm sorry to hear that. I loved them all and have missed my conversations with Tony. Bless him, he always tried to pound things into my thick skull, but I refused to learn anythin', I'm thinkin'."

"He loved you...they all did, but he missed you the most."

"He was smarter than new suspenders, but what the happy hell are you doin' here?"

She had tears in her eyes and said, "I came to be with you like you always were there for us whenever we needed you. I am truly sorry for your loss Jack, and I'm here for support if I can be of

134

help. I came here to the hotel instead of straight to the ranch. I didn't know how I would be received by your wife's family. I did not wish to intrude."

As he sat down in a chair he said, "That's kind of you, but you always were the sweetest lass around, a bit testy at times, but sweet, I'm tellin'. But a woman travelin' alone ain't fittin'. Don't you know how dangerous it is out there?"

She grinned and shook her head, "Knot-head! It is not like it was. One of my men drove me to San Tomas where I caught a train straight to Juarez. A trip that used to take days; now takes only hours. Aren't you glad to see me?"

"I'll be a two-headed yellow spider if I can think of anythin' that would please me more."

She laughed for several seconds before she said, "That's precious. I haven't heard that in years. It really takes me back. I've missed you knot-head! Come and tell me all about yourself. It's been twelve years since we've talked."

They talked for hours filling each other in on everything that had happened since they last talked. He hem-hawed around his lack of courage for not telling her in person of his marriage to Anna, but she let him off the hook by teasing that she may have shot him on the spot if he had. The news that affected him the most was how Delia was killed by a stray bullet when two drunks got in a shootout. She purposely left out the part where she was hit in the throat and took several hours to die. That would have served no purpose. She was aware that he knew the woman, her wranglers told of seeing him there from time to time, but she had no idea what their relationship actually was and didn't want to know for that matter. He tried to not let Carolina see the sudden sadness in his eyes, and if she noticed, she didn't let on.

She finally got around to the main reason for her trip, "Jack, I'm so very glad that you are no longer associated with the government. I never could see you as a rurale, but I'm sure you had your reasons, but Diaz has the people of this country at each other's throat and is losing control daily. I know you have your own hacienda now, but I need you too. I never thought I would grovel like I am, but I need your help. I have fought it until I no longer have the strength. I will never be able to hold on to my hacienda without your help. Come and live with me...I'm begging Jack! I hate myself for being so weak, but I love you damn it!"

He was breathless. He thought long and hard about what his next words should be. Finally he said, "That was the most powerful thing I've ever heard. I know the guts that took seein' as how proud you are and all. Do you remember that day you told your daddy that you'd just marry me and to hell with him? And how I said the next time you asked had better be sweeter? Do you remember?" She nodded, and he continued, "Well lass, that was the sweetest bunch of words ever spoke on god's green earth, I'm tellin'."

A look of great elation exploded on her face and she jumped up and said, "You will?"

"Of course! Hell, I'd of done it that very day if you hadn't of been so goddamned mean!" he laughed.

She rushed to him and kissed him long and hard. He lifted her and carried her to the bed and took her. She had saved her virginity all these years and now gave it willingly to the only man she had ever loved, or ever would. He was aware and appreciative of the gift she had given him. It was the second time in his life he had be so honored, the first being Anna. They both lay with tears in their eyes before they slept. Maybe God wasn't done with him after all.

Chapter Twenty-Two

Jack returned to his hacienda the next morning and told Reyes that he was going to the Salcido ranch to help an old friend with a problem with banditry and probably would not be back for quite a while. Reyes did not voice his disappointment, but his eyes told it. He sensed the real reason behind Jack's trip was Carolina herself. He felt Jack had a right to whatever happiness he could wrest from life, but he missed his daughter and this was a betrayal of sorts to her memory. He defeated these thoughts with the notion that Anna would never have wanted Jack to spend his life alone and would have approved. The two men hugged and Reyes had a man accompany Jack to Juarez to bring back the horse. As he waved from the porch of the house, he knew they would not meet again. He fought valiantly, but he broke down and sobbed. The singular exemplar of manhood he had ever known just rode out of his life.

On the train trip home, she said they should have a small private wedding at the ranch with only a few friends, but Jack insisted on a large one at the church in San Tomas. He reasoned that a wedding is the most important event in a woman's life and she deserved the biggest one he could muster. He remembered the comment Margarita once made as they had planned theirs, that the marriage was for the husband but the wedding was for the bride. Besides, his ego was compelled to show off for the townsfolk for their taking him as one of their own. She relented and a large wedding was planned for the following weekend. It wasn't a sacrifice since from childhood on she had always dreamed of a large wedding anyway…all girls did.

For appearances sake and to avoid Carolina's embarrassment in front of the servants, he spent the days running up to the wedding in a guest room at opposite ends of the upper floor of the house. They even remained celibate during this time for the same reasons, but also to add excitement for their wedding night. It was too late for it to be the first time, but it enhanced the expected intensity for the next time.

The news spread like wildfire and several hundred people crowded the square in front of the church. It was decided quickly to hold the services on the steps of the church so everyone could witness their favorite man marry the state's most powerful woman.

As the services were about to begin, he realized that he did not have a best man. He looked about the crowd quickly and spied Gustavo Ruiz. He motioned for the man to come to him and said, "Lad you look familiar and you're the only face I recognize in this mob. I've seen you somewhere before, I think, but would you do me the favor of being my best man? The job is easy I'm thinkin', all you have to do is stand there lookin' serious and shoot the bride if she tries to run," he grinned.

Surprised, he said, "Of course Senor Rose. It would be a great honor. I was in the crowd that day you shot those three men in this very square, but Senor Rose, I could never shoot so beautiful of a woman. God forbids it I'm sure," he laughed.

After the ceremony, a great celebration began. Many of the cafes were quickly pressed into serving what refreshments they could provide the crowd on short notice. After the drinking began, several guns were discharged in the air. Jack looked at Carolina and said, "I wish they wouldn't do that. When I hear that nonsense, I think someone's shootin' at me. I'd hate for some prominent townsfolk to get his ass shot off by mistake."

As they readied for bed on their first night of marriage, Carolina looked at her new husband and was brought to tears with

138

happiness. It had been a long time coming and now it had happened. She was Senora Carolina Rose. She laughed to herself as she thought of how she was the second Senora Rose and how there will never be a third because she'll shoot him herself if he ever tried to leave while she lived.

After lovemaking, she lay on her back in rapture as he scratched her ever so lightly from ankles to earlobes. She had no idea her body could feel as blissful as this. She had had her first climax and had no idea at the time what was happening to her. His soft caressing of her hypersensitive skin caused another orgasm leaving her exhausted and spent. Drained, she regretted all of those years of abstinence since celibacy had cost her this wave after wave of pure pleasure. She wondered where he had learned to do what he was doing but would never dream of asking. That was one of those questions, no matter how curious one may be, they really do not want to know. She decided it didn't really matter since she was getting the benefit of his knowledge. She put the idea out of her head of other women showing him where the "buttons" were. He was pleasuring her and that is what she needed to concentrate on.

Finally she opened her eyes and said, "That was wonderful. That little trick you just did was perfect." She could not help herself, as she sneakily phrased it that way to see if she could loosen any of his secrets. He always boasted of every other thing he had ever done, maybe he would pat himself on the back this time and let slip where he had gained all of his experience. Even though only part of her really did not want to face the answer, the other part was eaten by compelling curiosity. She wondered if all women went through this mental torture. Totally sated, her power of speech was reduced to merely a soft, throaty moan.

"Like it do you lass?" he asked as he continued caressing her wonderfully sexy body. "It's somethin' that came to me just this very minute." She knew that was a lie, it had to be, but she let him continue, "It gives me an excuse to lay here admiring a great work of art, I'm tellin'. You should see you from here by God! I'll be a two-headed yellow spider if you ain't magnificent lass" he grinned.

Suddenly struck by insecurity she asked, "Did you really like it? Were you really pleased?"

He looked down at her and smiled, "No knot-head, I always nearly faint for no goddamned reason! Of course you please me. Every thought of you pleases me. I love you Carolina, I really do. Since that very first day I saw you naked at the river, I dreamed of this very minute. If I hadn't of been so downright stupid, I'd of had a dozen years to have showed you by now. So no more silly questions, alright?"

"It's just that this is new to me. What you just did to me was magnificent, but I don't know what I'm doing. I want to be a good wife and please you, so be kind."

"Well whatever it is you don't think you know how to do, just keep not knowin' by God. I wasn't bangin' the headboard with my face because I'm thinkin' I'm too pretty!"

They made love again before they slept, and then again in the morning when they awoke. She had a brief gnawing fear that she may not survive the intensity and frequency of their lovemaking from what she had seen so far. She had nothing to compare it with, but she doubted if any other man could possess such raw power and manly appetites. She wasn't sure she was going to live through a lifetime of their lovemaking, but it promised to be an exciting way to go. Oddly, she remembered back to a time years earlier when she had overheard two wranglers talking of a third who had died while making love with his wife. They said euphemistically that he had "died with a smile on his face." She suddenly got it.

Over the next few years, the hacienda profited even more and Carolina's wealth grew great. She was deliriously happy. She had the man of her dreams who was turning out to be a good horseman as well. She turned over the job of selecting new breeding stock, the most important part of the ranches' operation and he flourished in his responsibilities.

He adored her and thought of Anna less and less until her memory was rare. He often felt bad that he had not contacted Reyes since the day he left, but he hoped the man would understand. He knew it would be the height of cruelty to be blissfully happy with his new life in the man's presence. He feared he would not have much to talk about other than his wife. Every event in his life centered round the hacienda and it seemed that he began every sentence with "my wife thinks this," or "Carolina says that." If he could not talk about Carolina or his work on her hacienda, he would not have much to say, and Reyes did not deserve that rudeness. By that time, he felt embarrassed he had let so many months go by without contacting Reyes in any manner—not even a single letter. But when Nacio wired him with the news that his longtime friend Alvaro Silva had been killed making an arrest, he was compelled to attend the funeral out of respect. Afterward, he spent a week with Reyes and his sons reestablishing their bonds. He vowed to keep in touch, but he never again had any further contact with the humble and good man.

One thing that brought frequent laughs to the couple was the idea that since the wedding day, not one horse had been stolen from the hacienda. He chuckled as he often asked, "Reckon why that is?" patting himself on the back.

She would always smile as she gave the same answer, "If you were in their place, would you steal from you, knot-head?"

For appearances sake, she began to have extravagant parties fairly regularly for the other hacienda owners as befitting her position as the most powerful woman in the state. With spies everywhere, she felt she must put as much distance possible between herself and "barefooted ones." Prominent town's people were also invited including his best man, Gustavo Ruiz.

The two men soon became great friends and Ruiz even took to asking Jack's advice on the area's military matters. He enjoyed Jack's tongue-in-cheek pat answer, "Lad, Theo Johns, the man who taught me to be a man always said, 'dead men have no further intentions'". A time or two, he even offered Porfirio Diaz's often quoted, "A little cannon smoke was not such a bad thing." Ruiz thought that of course Jack Rose would have an answer that involved somebody shooting something at someone. That's just who he was.

Ruiz really liked Jack but in his heart, he was a little jealous of him. He was rich beyond his own understanding, a friend of the president, and married to the most beautiful woman he had ever seen. God had smiled on the gunman beyond all measure of comprehension. But friends they were, and he would do anything within his power for the couple.

Part IV
The Last Act

Chapter Twenty-Three

Owing to the competitive nature of any organization, a man must have a guardian angel within that organization protecting him from the guardian angels of other men. This person of higher standing may not always open doors for his protégé, but ensures that at least they are not locked. This way the person of higher standing assures himself that those under him are loyal due to their dependence upon him.

Gustavo Ruiz entered the office to receive the insignias of his new rank of Major given to him in a by his guardian angel, General Victoriano Huerta. He was rapidly rising to the top and by far outstripping the others of his graduating class at Chapultepec. The only one at headquarters climbing the career ladder faster was Huerta himself. The general had his own guardian angel, Porfirio Diaz. Diaz needed no guardian angel, he had the army, which given the nature of things was much better.

Huerta shook the new major's hand and motioned for him to stand at ease. He returned to his seat behind his massive desk where he felt he looked his most impressive. He pulled some papers from the desk and said to Ruiz, "These are the reports you have sent me for the last year from the San Tomas and Chihuahua areas. The one name you mentioned most often is the bandit Pancho Villa. It would seem that he is a growing menace becoming even bolder the more followers he attracts. He and his band of rabble could easily become the most formidable of armies."

"But general," Ruiz began, "his army, if it could be called one, is mostly unarmed barefooted indigenous peasants. They are hardly an army sir. They are content with drinking tequila and singing songs of long lost loves. Villa rides from village to village marrying woman after woman. It is unclear what number wife he is on at present, but he has never divorced his first one so it doesn't matter. But that is what they are about mi general."

"Major, may I remind you that I am ethnic Huichol myself and know very well what the determination and industry of indigenous peoples can produce. As for being unarmed, how many guns can they acquire if they ambush and defeat a detachment of the army, and then another, and yet another? How many guns are these? Until now, they have contented themselves with just talk. But as in all things, talk must lead to action lest those being led find they have been misled, yet our president refuses to see that his dalliance emboldens these bandits…and that is all they are…Villa is a thug, nothing more. He and his ilk have spent their lives stealing small amounts but now see the opportunity to steal a country. They should be slapped down immediately before they become emboldened, but what does Diaz do? He has parades in the capital where he walks among the people smiling and shaking hands thinking that will make the peasants forget the footprints on their backs. The rural poor and under-classes are ignored at our peril. The only contact Diaz actually has with the people is with those of the middle class which are his already. There is no hunger in the bellies of the urban proletariat and they depend on him to keep it that way. The only crowds that turn out are those that would have been there to begin with."

Ruiz studied the general's face and mannerisms. Clearly, the man trusted him or he wouldn't be disparaging the president so openly. The clerks and aides hovering about in the outer offices must likewise be trusted since it was obvious they were within earshot and the general made no pretense at whispering. He felt he knew where the conversation was headed and his next question confirmed it, "Well, what is to be done mi general?"

"The president has recruited so much foreign investment to improve industry and technologies that the country virtually belongs to foreigners and not Mexicans. American companies alone own over twenty-five percent of the country. Soon even the dirt they will throw on top of our graves will not be ours. And have you seen this?" he retrieved a copy of some recent comments made by Diaz himself. "It says, and I quote, 'What this country needs is a new type of laborer. One who is not so intelligent and self-contained, but more obedient, industrious...and so forth.' He has already placed radical labor unions under government control and is encouraging immigration to develop the countryside. The same countryside, I might add, that he has divested of the population of farmers and farm workers by forcing them into the factories, mills and mines! First he runs everybody off the land; then he grovels at the feet of the Americans begging for money to develop this selfsame land in order to attract men to come work it. This means that in his mind, he has finally reached the conclusion that the underclass is no longer relevant and no longer poses any sort of threat to his government. Soon we will be up to our armpits with barefooted ones with machetes, or worse, brand new rifles given to them by Villa's American gun salesmen. There is no lack of those weasels."

"And what do you suggest mi general?" he knew this man would have a plan already in mind that would be both devious and beneficial to his own agenda.

"I think the assassination of a renowned local personage should suffice, don't you?"

"Villa?"

"No, no-one could not get close enough for that. His band of ragamuffins would tear the assassin to shreds. And just who could we get to volunteer for that? It would be a guaranteed suicide mission. What I have in mind is much easier to accomplish. I have in mind the assassination of the one person that would guarantee the desired response."

"Rose?" he asked hesitatingly, hoping he was not hearing correctly.

"Who better?" the general smiled. "The man suits our purposes as if we had created him ourselves for this reason alone."

"Begging the general's pardon, if you think killing Villa would be suicide, think ten times worse for the one who tries to assassinate Jack Rose."

"Major, it is not his death I seek; it is his wife's. If she were murdered, it would set in motion events that would only end in the destruction of her assailant. He is a violent and relentless man who would not stop until her death had been avenged. In this case, the evidence would lead to the desk of the president himself. To ensure this, there must be ample evidence that the deed was done by the army. There must be no confusion in his mind and for that I have something for you to leave near the body. It is a Presidential Pardon for the acts of reprisal against this list of traitors. It has been folded dozens of times to look as though it has been in a man's pocket for several days. Most of the names are of nonexistent people, but you will notice the Senora Rose is prominently mentioned. It must be left by the body to seem as if it had accidentally fallen out of your pocket."

His legs unwilling to support him further, Ruiz plopped down in a chair. He had just been given an order that was against everything he had ever believed in. His life was the army and he loved everything about it. Soldiers are called on to kill men in wars, but not murder innocent civilians to start wars, especially women. Because of the machinations, it was the most revolting order he had ever been given.

He also started to digest that he had just been given an order that may result in his own death…no…it would positively result in his own death if bungled. How could he possibly get in the position to kill the wife of the most dangerous and deadliest man ever to breathe the air of Mexico? He had seen the man in action and knew what he was capable of. Besides, he liked and respected the man and had become something of a friend over the years. He also had great fondness for his wife. She had always treated him as a well liked friend of the family.

It was at this moment that Ruiz realized that what he had suspected for years was in fact true. Huerta was positively disloyal, and worse, he was insane. He was willing and eager, to sacrifice the lives of thousands of men on both sides to further some diabolical plan to supplant the president. This would just be the first step in such a plan and Ruiz was expected to be the facilitator.

Huerta stared at Ruiz and thought the man looked as if he had just been stricken with an incurable disease, which in a way he had, and asked, "Is there a problem major? The look on your face tells me that you think I have just given you an impossible order. Of course it won't be easy, heroic missions never are, but the woman knows you well enough to trust you in her presence. Who else around here can make that claim? What could be more innocent than wanting to show a friend your new rank?"

Ruiz pondered his next move. He was torn between shooting himself to save Jack Rose the effort and shooting the diabolical Huerta to save Mexico the effort. He knew that he would do neither, but it was a thought…a fleeting desperate thought…but still just a thought. He asked to be excused because he had a train north to catch and plans to make.

Ruiz took his leave and went home to say goodbye to his wife. He looked at her as though he was seeing her for the last time. He felt that in this instance, it just may be true. Looking into her eyes, he knew that the mad man would have her killed if he refused to obey his orders. The bastard would not hesitate for one minute. He was trapped and resigned himself to his fate.

She sensed something troubling in his manner, but would never think to ask, and he would never think to tell. For the first time in her life, she saw tears in his eyes.

* * * *

On what he feared might be the last day of his life, Gustavo Ruiz rose from a fitful night. He basically had had no sleep. The walls of his small room had spent the night inching closer to his bed until they seemed to physically impair his breathing. But that was of little consequence since he had nearly forgotten how to breathe anyway due to his terror of what the day's action offered.

He spent his morning in short-tempered scolding of his men for any misstep, no matter how slight. It was so against his natural temperament that they could not help but notice and grumbled among themselves. He had never raised his voice to any of his men. He was not that kind of officer.

At the noon break, he mounted and rode for the ranch some eight miles distant. He knew that Jack was always out on the range at this time of day. He found Carolina alone in the house preparing to go out. She was glad to see him and asked why he was there in the middle of the day. He offered an excuse of wanting to see Jack on some business. He asked for a glass of water before he was to ride out on the range to look for him.

As they chatted idly about the recent activities in San Tomas, he compulsively fingered the folded paper in his shirt pocket. His hands shook from nerves and unnoticed by him, the paper fell to the floor. He walked to the window to enjoy the view of the valley below and the mountains in the distance. She had seen the paper fall near his chair and while he stood there at the window, Carolina retrieved the paper from the floor. She made an inadvertent gasp when she read her name.

He saw her reflection in the window and spun around humiliated that she had seen the list before he had readied himself. He reached for his pistol, but unbuttoning the holster flap was nearly impossible with trembling hands. When he finally succeeded in pulling his weapon, she already hers in hand from the thigh holster under her dress. She fired hitting him in the left eye, blowing off the back of his head. He fell with a thud. He twitched twice and was then no more.

She was still sitting at the table stunned when Jack came in minutes later. He said, "Where's Gus? That's his horse out front. Where'd the lad get to?"

She didn't say a word merely pointed to his body at the front window.

"Christ on the cross, what happened?" he asked as he saw Ruiz's weapon in his hand. He examined it and saw that it had not been fired. He saw that his left eye had been blown out and said, "You missed. If you were aimin' for between the eyes, you were off by about two inches."

"Shut up!" she snapped in no mood for his silliness. She handed him the paper and said, "He dropped this by accident. He didn't see me read it so I was prepared when he made his move. I don't think he expected me to react like I did. I only had my holster on because I was going in to San Tomas this afternoon. He died with a look of great surprise on his face. But I just can't believe that Diaz would put me on a list for reprisal. I have done nothing to deserve this."

He shook his head and said, "This ain't Diaz's work. This has Huerta's smell all over it. The president would give a verbal order to avoid havin' it on paper to trace back to him. He ain't that stupid, and besides, I would be the target and not you. But that som-bitch Huerta is a back-shootin' rat and would murder you to make me mad enough to kill Diaz. That way he could just waltz in as pretty as you please all innocent and such."

She was amazed her husband's mind worked through the gyrations behind Ruiz's attempt on her life. She agreed wholeheartedly with his observations. If Diaz was the behind the plot, he would have Jack killed because he is a man to be feared. But Huerta on the other hand would use Jack's rage to have Diaz killed rather than implicate himself in some presidential assassination plot. Her real concern became the fear that her husband would board a train for the capital and blow a very big hole in the chief conspirator.

Jack sat for the longest time staring at the lifeless body of his friend. He finally muttered out loud, "Gus, you silly som-bitch. You must'a known you had about as much of a chance of pullin' this off as I do of becomin' the recordin' angel. Goin' after my wife? You had to know you were outmatched. You knew her history. You've seen her shoot! But I admire your guts lad, I really do. You had no chance, but you didn't shoot her in the back like a coward! You were too good and decent of a man for that, but why'd you let that bastard Huerta talk you into this silly shit? Goddamn it lad, goddamn it!" He actually shed a tear.

He tied the body across Ruiz's horse and led him back to the garrison. He stopped at the gate without entering and shouted to the gathering men, "This was a good man. You were lucky to have known him, treat him with respect and tell that som-bitch Huerta to come himself next time! He'll know what you mean. And tell him to come after me; he damned sure ain't good enough to tangle with my wife!"

At home, he found Carolina quietly sobbing as she cleaned the blood from the floor. He wanted to comfort her but he didn't know what to say...so he said nothing.

The incompetence of the chosen agent of her death had cost him his life instead. 1899 wasn't such a good year for Gustavo Ruiz after all. Though still many years in the future, one might say the first shot of the revolution had been fired, and its first victim had been felled.

Chapter Twenty-Four

Jack was shown into the president's office in his private train car where he found the man seated behind his desk. He was pleased that the man seemed actually happy to see him as stood and offered his hand. This was special treatment for the president did not usually do so. As the one with all of the power, he always let the visitor do the fawning. Jack returned the handshake and noticed that the man's face had aged since their last meeting, but change was expected after nearly twenty years. However what attracted the most attention were the president's eyes. All of those years earlier, the man's eyes were bright and inquisitive. Now they were ringed, dark and piercing. He wondered what he himself would look like after twenty years of the pressures this man had faced.

As Jack took a seat, the president nodded to a servant to begin pouring coffee for both. The president thanked the servant and looked at Jack as he began, "My dear friend Jack. How many years has it been?"

Jack grinned and replied, "This old body of mine says it must have been a hundred, easy."

The president laughed and agreed and turned serious, "My friend, you have made an enemy of Huerta. It seems you have foiled his plan to have you assassinate me. He is quite angry I would guess."

"Excellency, he is the one who angered me. I am guessin' that you know about his attempt on my wife's life?"

"It was an amateurish plan at best. If he wanted my death, he could have made the attempt on me directly. He could have had his pick from any number of assassins; the good Lord knows there are plenty who would volunteer. But he wanted us both. He wished to have you arrested as you stood over my dead body. He has feared you since the day we all met on my train. He warned me about you several times over the years. I don't know why he hates you so; maybe it is because you could never be controlled."

"He's a weasel, and I owe him."

The president shook his head and said, "That is why I have asked you to see me today. I wish to ask you to not plan revenge against him at this time. He has a large faction of the army's generals that would back him in a coup. Any attempt on his life might be the spark to set them off. As you say, he is a weasel and plots to seize power, but at this time, I don't trust enough officers to have that fight. Everyone at the palace thinks you and I are friends since they all have seen the photograph your wife sent me of your wedding. It sits on the table behind my desk among other prized ones. If you kill him, it may look as though I ordered you to do it, since you are a man of such repute."

"Well I'll be a two-headed yellow spider! You tell me not to kill the man who tried to murder my wife to make me kill you in return because it may piss off a bunch of back stabbin' traitors? Excellency, that's a bit over my head. I would think that you'd want his head splattered all over some wall."

"I do, but not at this time. I cannot afford to divide the army now, because revolution is in the air. It is not noticed, but over the years I have reduced the size of the army to less than fourteen thousand and many of those left may not be so forgiving and loyal. I have trade unions, anarchists, ultra-liberal newspapers, disgruntled churchmen and all sorts of other rebellious elements nipping at my heels. And I have Francisco Madero leading this chorus calling for my head. Like I said, I don't have the wherewithal for that battle just now. So please honor my wishes if you will. Of course, I cannot tell a man how to avenge his wife, but I'm asking."

Jack got up and paced a bit before finally saying, "Excellency, you're puttin' a bunch of pressure on me. I have promised God to destroy this man. Also, the assassin he sent was a friend, but so are you, so I'll delay God's own justice until you say I can be blowin' holes in that som-bitch. So, just as soon as you decide I can send that weasel through hell's front door, let me know and we'll both piss on his grave!"

"Agreed! That is something we can do together. I promise, and please give my compliments to the beautiful senora. Tell her I am sorry that affairs keep me from visiting the daughter of my old friend. Maybe soon, I can take some time for myself. We will get drunk and tell lies."

Jack grinned and said, "Excellency, I'm Irish as you know, so I'm thinkin' you'll be in over your head in this one, by god. My sainted mother once told me, my first words were a bald face lie, and I'm thinkin' I ain't got any more truthful since."

The president stood to offer his hand and said, "My dear Jack, have you forgotten that I'm a politician? No-one would ever vote for a man that cannot tell convincing lies."

Jack got up and shook hands with the president and left his personal car. As he walked to his horse, he thought to himself that he still liked the man no matter what the newspapers and scallywags about town may say. He was a good man with bad men snipping at him. He just worried if his wife would understand his delay in escorting Huerta off the planet. She hadn't said anything of that possibility, but she would know his honor code demanded it.

Jack sat down at the table and told Carolina about his visit with the president. He told of the request to forestall any vengeance on his part towards Huerta. She agreed with the president. Vengeance may set unstoppable events in motion that the country was not yet ready for. The army was rife with disloyal elements. He then took her hands in his and said, "No man comes after you and lives to tell about it, but I'll wait for now. Know this, if it costs me every drop of my blood, me and that viper will cross hell's gate with my hands around his throat. God demands it. He's tellin' me so right this minute!"

Chapter Twenty-Five

For half of the next decade, Jack kept his promise to Carolina and the president and forestalled his vengeance against Huerta. He never forgot and he would never forgive. He was philosophically unable to ignore an insult such as the attempt on his wife's life, but he was able to bide his time. Like the old adage, "revenge was a dish best served cold."

He contented himself with his work on the ranch, especially riding the property to be seen in case any undesirables were afoot with plans of mischief. The sameness of his routine made the weeks melt into months and then into years without much variation.

His well noted stubbornness was never more evidenced as by his refusal to learn to drive Carolina's new Oldsmobile. She had spent a few days in Chihuahua visiting an elderly aunt and bought the vehicle. There were several on the road there and even a few in San Tomas so she decided it was time for one in the family. She also ordered a flatbed truck for use on the ranch. She drove up to the house and told Jack to get in for a quick ride about the place.

He stated flatly, "If God had wanted men to drive, he would have never created horses, I'm thinkin'."

She laughed and said, "Knot-head, it is OK with God since he allowed someone to invent it in the first place. You ride on trains all of the time and they are not mentioned in the bible anywhere. So don't be a caveman and get in damn it!"

"No! It ain't fittin' for a woman to drive anyway! I've had my say!"

"John Jack Rose, you get in this car right now...I've had my say!"

He relented, as usual, and enjoyed the ride despite himself, but he held the line on learning to drive himself. Mechanical devices had always defeated him and he knew he would never get the hang of having to use his feet on something with pedals. She thought about it as well and agreed that he would be a disaster behind the wheel so she dropped her demand. She smiled at him and said, "I guess you are fine with been seen in town with a female chauffeur? Do you want people to say, 'there go the Roses, she must wear the pants in the family?' That's what they will say you know."

"Hell lass, they say that now. Everyone has known you since the day you were born and know what your temperament is, I'm thinkin'. They all know that you're the only thing with a pulse that I'm afraid of by God! I'm your pet thug and everyone knows that. Besides, do you actually think someone is goin' to make some smart-assed comment when we drive by?"

He loved his wife to distraction and spent as much time as possible in her presence just drinking in her beauty. He never tired of looking at her. For her part, she never tired of his attention. Even after nineteen years of marriage, they still acted like newlyweds. They held hands in public and cuddled nightly by the fireplace. They had long since stopped making love as frequently as before, but for a man in his late sixties, it was to be expected. He would try occasionally but would be embarrassed if he failed. He was not a man who took failure easily. However, he kept her satisfied with his stroking techniques and for her that was good enough. For her part, she would return the favor as best as she could so anything more on either's part was not missed.

Carolina continued to monitor the political situation and became increasingly more open in her growing opposition to the Diaz regime like other economically vulnerable elites of the region who began to demand more political influence. In 1908 and 09, the corn and cotton failures in Chihuahua and other states as well as the bottoming out of the world silver market led to the overall collapse of mining in general and produced massive unemployment with mine, timber, and farm workers seeking refuge in impossibly overcrowded cities and towns in the north. Reduced railroad and port activities reflected the decline in these important industries. The final blow was when the US government imposed a high tariff on sugar imports in an attempt to protect the American producers in Cuba. Diaz felt the market would restore itself and refused for the government to go into debt. No funds were made available for relief for the landless rural working class, small businessmen and urban poor, and famine soon tracked down this dispossessed population.

She didn't discuss any of these developments with Jack mainly because he had no interest, that, and he was a friend of the president. He didn't wish to hear any negative comments because he was nothing if not loyal. He had a glare that was an effective deterrent to unwanted political discourse. Friends and acquaintances knew this look and his fondness for the president and avoided any such talk.

One morning Jack sat down at the table to have his coffee with Carolina when a servant of the household broke into the room with a newspaper she had just picked up that morning in San Tomas while shopping for supplies. Carolina's face turned ashen as she read the single word headline—Revolution! She looked at her husband and said softly, "It has begun."

She leaned back in her chair as she slid the paper across the table to Jack. He read aloud the story that the shooting war began when a stockpile of arms was found at the home of a Madero sympathizer, the Serdan family in Puebla. It read that in Chihuahua, a force of farmers and farm workers, cowboys, miners, and peasants were following Pascual Orozco, including the notorious Pancho Villa.

Jack laid the paper down and looked at Carolina and said, "I guess this means that El Jefe is in it now. Lass, you know I don't keep up with this shit all that close, but what got everybody to shootin'? Why is everyone so pissed at the president? He's done nothin' but try to make somethin' out of these ignorant lowlife's. He gets kicked in his teeth for the effort!"

She smiled at her husband and tried to keep the explanation at the most basic level and said, "Do you remember hearing the name Francisco Madero?"

"Vaguely; Diaz said somethin' about him I think; isn't he that lawyer rat you said was stirrin' everything up?"

"Yes, that's him," she started, "Diaz had him put under house arrest from there he escaped and fled to Texas. He put out a document called the 'Plan of San Lois Potosi' where he promised democracy, worker's rights, and land reform. Foreigners own ninety percent of our economy and 150 million acres of our land. Diaz's economic plan of expansion regardless of consequences was responsible for such a disgraceful situation. That's why I told you before that I was afraid that the people would be easily led under those conditions, and I'm right; it has begun. The people want more voice in the running of their country. I never told you, but for the last several years my sympathies have come around to their side in this, but now we do have a problem. Large estates will be confiscated and ours in particular will be targeted being known friends of the president."

Jack snarled, "Let'em try! Me, and some of the lads will blow them som-bitches to hell for their efforts!"

"It's not as simple as that. If they win the war, they will confiscate our lands through the courts. Otherwise, they will simply invade us, steal everything of value, and kill any of us still here. That is the nature of bandit armies."

"Well I don't care which group of bastards show up wantin' some shit, I'll be stackin' 'em up like cordwood. They may get me, but I'll gather a goddamned bunch of ghosts to take with me. Hide and watch to see if I don't!"

"Don't be ridiculous. Even the great Fast Jack Rose in his prime couldn't stop an army, and sweetheart, you are no longer in your prime. But hear me out; I want you to go into San Tomas to the bank and have all of our money wired to...where do you think we should go...San Antonio, Houston, New Orleans? Make it New Orleans. Have everything wired to a bank in New Orleans, that way when things get out of control, we can still survive."

He agreed with the soundness of her idea and rode to town to take care of business.

As he neared the house upon his return, he saw what looked like bodies. As he raced towards the scene, he saw that they were in fact bodies. He counted a dozen before he saw one particular body that was a knife to his heart. Carolina was curled up on the bottom step of the veranda. She was dead, shot several times including many in the back. By her side lay the body of the gardener, poor old Senor Podesta. By the looks of things, they had acquitted themselves well.

He sat in the dirt and cradled her head in his lap. He let out a primal scream followed by a scathing attack on God, "If you're so fuckin' pissed at me, kill me damn it and leave the women the hell alone. You've killed every goddamned one that I ever loved! They've done nothin' to you but you're so petty and pissed off at me about somethin', you ain't actin' right!"

Once again under control, he apologized, "I'm sorry for that silly shit just now. It's just that I don't understand why every woman in my life has to go and die so goddamned young...pardon me God...but why are you so pissed at me?...amen."

He brushed the hair away from her face and sobbed for the rest of the afternoon and into the evening. He sat there holding her and talking to her in the gentlest of tones. He apologized for every incident in their married life that had caused her aggravation or sadness, or anything at all that had caused an emotion other than complete happiness and contentment. Several times he would look towards heaven and beg God to love her and shine his face upon her and whatever other words from the benediction he could remember. He told her dozens of times just how proud of her he was. Since Podesta did not have a gun, she obviously had gotten all twelve of the murdering horse thieves by herself. "You did good lass," he said out loud. "You got twelve of them som-bitches before they got you. Those bastards are this minute in hell pleadin' with Satan for a drink of water and you're in heaven tellin' ole Saint Peter just how things need to be done, by God! Judgin' by your empty belt, if you hadn't of run out of bullets, you'd still be killin' rats even now! You can rest assured that when I catch the bastards, I'll make them regret...forgive me...I know you don't like hearin' it...but I'll make them regret that their daddies ever mounted their mommas. If you think I won't, you just keep lookin' down from heaven and see if I don't!"

He sat in that position until just before daylight when he had to set her down to step away to answer nature.

Soon what few wranglers that were still on the ranch, rode up from where they were hiding from the attackers. The men were horrified at what they saw. They were grief stricken at the scene. Jack told them to see to Podesta's body, while he carried hers into the house. He laid her on their bed and instructed the terrified and sobbing housekeeper to bathe and dress her before sending for the priest.

The men reported that the herd from the south valley was missing. He retrieved his Sharps from the gun rack and rode out to pick up the trail of the stolen horses. As he followed, he shouted, "Don't look back you bastards, hell's right behind you!"

The trail was easy to follow since a hundred horses leave markers. They led straight to Dos Paso's a small village ten miles due south of the ranch. He could see the animals in a temporary corral at the edge of the village. He didn't stop there but rode towards the gathering of men just ahead. He knew whose men they were. He continued riding deeper into Villa's camp to the roaring shouts of "El Condor, El Condor!" by the assembled revolutionaries. He followed the path the parting crowd made until he was in front of Villa himself. He dismounted and strode up to the man and snorted, "I've come to kill you, you bastard! You killed my wife and now's your turn! You're wearin' at least three pistols I can see from here, so grab one goddamn it!"

The crowd was stunned into silence when the men realized that the famous gunman was not joining their ranks, but had terrible intentions instead. Villa looked at him with the smile he was noted for as the sound of dozens of guns being cocked surrounded both men. He asked sarcastically, "You do know that you are outnumbered? There are many men at your back who will shoot you if you try anything."

"Them lowlifes seem to prefer shootin' people in the back like they did my wife, but she got twelve of your bastards before they got her, by God! Back-shootin' is for cowards and horse thief's and you, you som-bitch are the worst of the lot!"

Villa shook his head and said, "Are you really wanting to die that badly gringo? That's what will happen if you try anything."

"Hell, I ain't that worried about the 'tryin'' because I'm pretty damned good at the 'doin'! God's shoutin' in my ear that He's ready if I am!"

"Before you get us both killed, look there," he said pointing to the bodies of four men hanging from a nearby tree. "That man nearest to you was sent to your ranch to negotiate for the horses, but he decided to steal them instead. He had no integrity the bavoso, and deserved his fate. The other three could not convince me they were not the ones who shot the Senora. So I let God decide if they lied. The Senora defended her ranch better than most men would have done. She over matched my poor peons and acquitted herself with honor. She was much woman, and I'm sorry for your loss. I sincerely am."

Jack sighed and still angry said, "You'd have loved her, everybody did. She was actually on your side in this war and that's what makes this so tragic! If that stupid som-bitch had of asked, she's have given him every goddamned horse on the place. She started as a Diaz partisan, but came over to your side when she could no longer stomach the pain and suffering. She even kept her donations anonymous for fear of Diaz's spies."

"That is not so much of a worry anymore since we shoot all of the spies we catch."

"Yeah, that leads me to a question," Jack said, "if you shoot wrong doers in the army, why did you hang that bastard?" pointing at the dead man.

"We did that out of respect for you Senor Rose. Don't they hang horse thieves in your country? We thought you would appreciate the gesture."

"I do, but this has been my country for the past thirty years. Your pal Diaz made me a Mexican, don't I look like one?" he smiled.

"You are as Mexican as any of these son's of Cortez, El Condor" he teased.

"Please...call me Jack...I ain't no goddamned vulture. I hate that nickname, always have. My first wife called me that too, may the saints bless her."

"The people mean no disrespect. They say you once killed six men in San Tomas at one time...is that true my friend?"

"Why hell no, there was only three...and one of them put a bullet in my dumb ass! That was over thirty years ago and I was thinkin' I was bulletproof I guess. I'm now nearly sixty-eight and can't see well enough to do silly shit like that anymore...thank God! A lad could get himself shot up you know?"

"What, only three? How ordinary," Villa teased, "but do not worry, your secret is safe. I will leave them to their legends."

"Ordinary! I may not be able to be killin' three at a time anymore, but I sure as hell can get one!" he mocked as he pretended to reach for his pistol.

Villa got serious and asked, "Jack, where were you born?"

"Ireland...County Cork, Ireland."

"And why did you come here?"

"Here? You mean here in your camp?"

"No. I mean why did you come to the America's?"

"The bloody English were starvin' the Irish so many thousands had to come here to survive. Why?"

Villa continued, "Look around you Jack. These are my Irishmen and our English King sits in Mexico City and calls himself Porfirio Diaz. I need your help training these men. Most of them are poor ignorant peons who have never held a gun in their lives. Many hundreds of them are going to die when we go into battle, and the battle is coming soon. The army is on the trains even now. The shooting has already begun in Puebla. Will you help me to give them a chance to survive?"

"Pancho lad, were you not listening just now? I'm sixty-eight goddamned years old! I can't be chargin' around with guns a blazin'. Besides, I don't know anything about military tactics. I'm a retired hotheaded gunman, nothin' more."

"You know more than you think. When you fight a man, you always try to put him in a position of disadvantage don't you? A battle is just the same. You try to put their whole army at a disadvantage. But I'm not asking you to lead an army, just teach them how to shoot to stay alive. I'll do the leading."

Jack grinned and said, "I'm sorry jefe, but I have seen the absolute last body I have a care to. Most of them deserved it, some didn't, but when that precious woman died by the gun, I'll be god damned if I ever contribute to another person leavin' this tired planet, so help me God. With that he took off his gun belt and handed it to Villa telling him it was a gift from an admirer. He didn't know it for sure, but he doubted the man had ever gotten a gift quite like it. He was holding some violent history in his hands.

Villa told Jack that in honor of his wife, he was going to call his bravest unit of cavalry "Caroistas." He was touched by Villa's gesture and thought it ironic that a military unit of men going off to war against other men would be named for a woman who would have probably led them into that battle, had she been given the chance. He thought, "Knowing her, she'd be as proud as a new dollar."

Both men talked for another hour before they decided it was time to sleep. Both men would have plans to make; one for a battle the other for a funeral.

Chapter Twenty-Six

The president handed General Huerta a report and said, "So now it begins. Madero's minions have finally thrown away their speeches and have started throwing bombs. Before you say it, you were right. I should have shot him when I had the chance."

Huerta smiled but said nothing. The universal urge to say "I told you so," is great within men but in this case he had gotten the recognition he sought and that was sufficient. "Excellency, I have taken the liberty to draw up a plan of battle for your approval, of course. I propose that I take the army and begin the war against Zapata in the south. He is much more formidable a foe than Villa. Villa's army of the north is mostly bandits and will be concerned with stealing everything in sight and too busy to mount anything other than raiding parties. After Zapata has been dispatched, we can give El Bandito Grande his proper attention."

Diaz looked at the map he had been handed then said, "General, it is well and good that you concentrate first on Zapata since his army is close by and can be in the capital quickly if not confronted. But do not underestimate Villa. His army is the largest in Mexico and will be difficult to defeat. The area is much too vast to allow him freedom of movement. No, general, I wish you to send half of the army north. If Villa links up with Carranza and Orozco we may as well host their victory party ourselves."

"But Excellency, Carranza and Villa hate each other as much…"

"As they hate me?" Diaz continued the sentence for him.

Huerta blushed slightly and said, "I may have worded it better, but yes Excellency. They are as likely to shoot at each other as they are at us. But to gamble half of our army on the possibility that they don't may invite defeat. Dividing one's forces is never a good strategy. I still urge caution; Zapata should be first. What may I tell the commanders?"

"You can tell them that half of them are going north!" he snorted. He wasn't about to let a man hold sway whose last military assignment was re-designing the army's uniforms. He was a smart military mind himself and knew that if the northern army of Villa wasn't stopped, it would not matter any longer. He knew that if he didn't squeeze out a victory over both Villa and Zapata, his regime had, at best, a year left.

He was prophetic for on May 25, 1911, members of his government forced him to step down to prevent further bloodshed. He went into exile in Paris to spend the rest of his days with only his devoted Molina at his side. His parting words were, "Francisco Madero has unleashed a tiger; now let's see if he can tame it!" Time would bear him out and would show Madero could not.

Jack spent the next few years in seclusion in New Orleans, the place where he first set foot in the Americas. He read newspaper accounts of the revolution with great interest. He was amused that as soon as Madero became president, his coalition of generals fell apart into something of a civil war, especially between Carranza and Villa. Zapata was even sent packing into the mountains by his supporters. What he really could not abide was Huerta eventually rose to the presidency. He regretted that he had not gone to Mexico City to end that bastard's life like he had wanted. He thought to another time in his life when he had not acted and someone had died as a result. He knew that the people of Mexico would end up paying for his inaction...God had promised as much.

The world was tearing itself apart with the Great War. Europeans were killing other Europeans, while Mexicans were killing their own. France was particularly in it, especially near

Paris where his one time friend now lived. He was sure the president was safe and away from the fighting; that is the nature of presidents, even those who no longer wore the badge of office.

Jack sat in a deck chair bundled against the chill offered by the winds of the north Atlantic. He had heard a steward tell another passenger that the ship was about two hours out of Galway. He had said to keep an eye just over the bow and in an hour and a half Ireland would come into view. He said the ship was running at fourteen knots. Jack didn't know exactly what a knot was but he snorted to himself that he "wouldn't own a horse if he wasn't any faster than this goddamned barge!"

He had spent most of the morning reading the newspaper accounts of the Great War. Reports from the various hot-spots around the world told of men killed in the hundreds of thousands, and civilians also dying in horrendous numbers. Modern weapons enabled a single man to kill by the hundreds at a time. Machine guns, grenades, tanks, poison gas, artillery and even the newest implement of death, the airplane had taken honor and bravery out of men facing men in combat.

He was glad that his time in the world had passed and he had never faced nor used such fiendish weaponry. In his day, men had to face one another close enough to smell the breath of the other. The most sophisticated piece of technology he had ever used was his Sharps rifle and he wasn't proud of that at the time.

Before he quit the Americas, he had seen newspaper photos of what these weapons were capable of doing as they had surveyed the battlefields of a dozen clashes of armies. Dead men were stacked as high as a man is tall waiting for their turn to be tossed into common graves. Sickened by the graphic depictions of the carnage, he finally reached his limit of reading stories of men interviewed at night that would be dead in the morning and decided he would go to Ireland to live out his days in the land of his birth. He came to the conclusion that he had seen enough of a world that was too engrossed with killing its inhabitants. It was almost as if the earth was trying to rid itself of these pesky little pests scurrying about on its surface. All he now wanted was a quiet cottage near a stream and no word from anywhere past his property line. In the names of both of his wives, he donated millions of dollars to the church in New Orleans for the Mexican Relief Fund keeping only enough for his own purposes and set sail.

As he sat in his deck chair pondering these thoughts, the deck exploded under his feet and he was blown several feet into the air. He was dead when he hit the deck, a victim of the very modern weapons he detested. He had been killed by the most sophisticated and highly technical of man's killing devices of the age; a U-boat with a torpedo. In his wildest dreams, he would never have imagined such a thing could even exist. But exist it did, and it had ended the existence of an old man within sight of a home he had not seen in sixty-one years. He had led an exciting and full life and that life ended just a handful of watery miles short of coming full circle. He had left a penniless child but was returning a man, a man who was more than just a man—a legend. Yet, he would be mourned by but one. Reyes would learn of it several days later when he would see the El Paso newspaper's notice of "Notables" reported in the death of a ship off the coast of Ireland. He had fled to Texas after Villa's land reform took his property, and the regulares mistaking them for revolutionaries, took his sons.

At that exact hour in Paris many thousands of miles removed from the frightful revolution fought in his name and against his name, Porfirio Diaz lay on his deathbed. Both men had shared the same era in Mexico, but not the same air. One fell from the heights while the other would never have thought to seek such altitudes. One had gathered ghosts numbered in multiples of tens, and the other gathered ghosts numbered in multiples of thousands. They both would be remembered, one with stories told in history books, and the other with tales told around the dinner table. The captain of the U-boat murdered the man, but the legend will live as long as men tell their sons of the feats of brave men.

At 3:00 PM on July 2, 1915 both would pass from the scene. Millions would mourn Porfirio Diaz while Jack Rose would be mourned by only Reyes Antonio Garcia.

Thus was the remarkable life of John Jack Rose...the Ghost Gatherer...

Finale

In an interview in 1908, President Diaz remarked that Mexico was ready to be a democracy. Francisco Madero agreed and announced he would seek the presidency in the elections of 1910. Diaz was not as progressive as he had appeared and had Madero arrested and himself declared the winner. It was indeed, business as usual for the man who had retained power by hook or crook for thirty years.

On November 20, 1910, Madero published "Plan de San Luis Petosi," which called for the people of Mexico to rise up against Diaz. The thirty year dictatorship, the maltreatment of the poor, and the growing disparity between the rich and the poor were sited among the charges. Even though he was opposed to violence, he could see no other way to oust Diaz so he issued his call to arms.

On November 18, two days before the revolution was to start, a stockpile of arms was found at the Serdan family home and the first battle was fought then and there. It was now a shooting war and no longer a war of words.

On May 25, 1911, members of his government forced him to step down to prevent further bloodshed. He was exiled to Paris to spend the rest of his days.

As soon as Madero was installed as the new president, his coalition disintegrated. Madero was mostly interested in political changes while Zapata and Villa had been fighting for social justice and land reforms. Carranza defended the interests of the upper classes and was backed by the United States. To show his displeasure, Villa attacked Columbus, New Mexico suffering many casualties and incurred the pursuit back into Mexico by US General John J. Pershing. The alliance of Carranza and Alvaro Obregon defeated Villa and he was later assassinated in 1923.

Huerta's role as slithering snake behind the scenes was not ended with the abdication of Porfirio Diaz. He immediately offered his services to the new Madero administration and soon insinuated himself in deep enough to be charged with crushing anti-Madero revolts by rebel generals such as Pascual Orozco. All the while he was secretly plotting with US Ambassador Henry Lake Wilson, General Bernado Reyes and Felix Diaz, nephew of Porfirio, to overthrow Madero.

On February 18, 1913 he took Madero and vice president Jose Maria Pino Suarez prisoner. He promised the two men safe passage into exile. To give the appearance of legitimacy he had Foreign Minister Pedro Lascurain, constitutionally the next in line of succession, installed as the new president. Within the hour, Lascurain stepped down handing the presidency to Huerta. His armed thugs forced the congress to endorse his assumption of power. His first order of business was to have Madero and Pino Suarez shot. Reaction from Carranza, Villa, Obregon and Zapata was swift and after defeats of his army culminating at the battle of Zacatecas, he resigned on July 15, 1914.

He went into exile in Kingston, Jamaica then England, then Spain and finally the United States where it was discovered he had plotted with the agents of the German Kaiser Wilhelm II for another coup d'état. He was arrested in Newman, NM on June 27, 1915. He died of cirrhosis of the liver in prison at Fort Bliss on January 13, 1916. He was 65. He is vilified to this day as El Chacal—the Jackal...

About The Author

Until his eighteenth birthday, Raymond lived in Pittsburg, California where he was educated at PHS before returning to the city of his birth, Decatur, Alabama. Upon finishing school, he spent time in the United States Air Force where his last assignment was in Thailand. After leaving the service, he married and settled down in Birmingham, Alabama where he played music on the nightclub circuit for many years.Returning to Decatur, he attended nearby Athens State University earning a Bachelor's of Science Degree in Psychology where he was admitted to Psi Chi, the National Honor Society for Psychology. He attended Graduate School at the University of North Alabama in Florence.

He still lives in Alabama near his daughter and three grandchildren. He enjoys cooking Italian, and eating Mexican. He now writes full-time and although his first love is writing humor, he enjoys the studying and researching required for his work of Historical Fiction which he sees as challenging him to learn the cultures he writes about.

His goal is "To someday write something that matters."